HERO

Leslie McGill

SADDLEBACK
EDUCATIONAL PUBLISHING

CAP CENTRAL

Fighter
Running Scared
Hacker
Gearhead
The Game
Hero

EDUCATIONAL PUBLISHING
www.sdlback.com

ISBN-13: 978-1-68021-046-0
ISBN-10: 1-68021-046-7
eBook: 978-1-63078-352-5

Printed in Guangzhou, China
NOR/0615/CA21500931

19 18 17 16 15   1 2 3 4 5

To Nanny Annie, the world's best mom

CHAPTER 1

NINA

Charlie Ray threw his pencil down on the desk. "Seriously?" he complained.

Lights flashed in the hallway. A mechanized voice said, "There is an emergency in the building. Please proceed to the nearest exit."

"Mrs. Maher, can we just stay here?" Nina Ambrose asked. "You know it's another false alarm."

"Unfortunately, we can't," Mrs. Maher said. "If we're outside too long to finish the exam, I'll give you more time. Let's line up."

Nina put down her pencil and got in line with the rest of the class. She was in the middle of writing a long answer to an essay question on *The Grapes of Wrath*. She didn't want to lose her train of thought.

She picked up her purse and automatically checked to make sure she had a small notebook and a pen. As a reporter for the *Star*, Capital Central High School's online newspaper, she was always on the lookout for a good story.

"This stuff is starting to really scare me," Keisha Jackson said, walking beside Nina. "All these false alarms? And so many thefts lately. My phone last week. Marcus DiMonte's wallet. I've heard other kids have had stuff stolen too. It just seems like—oh my gosh! Is that smoke?"

The hallway was filling with smoke. Students started running. Some started pushing to get down the stairs.

Jair Nobles stood at the top of the stairwell. "Hey, chill!" he said to one boy who was racing to get around the crush of students. "You've got time. Take it easy. Don't want anybody to get hurt, man!"

"Hey, J!" Keisha said, stopping at the top of the stairs. Students tried to push past her. "This looks bad. You coming?"

"Yeah, I'm out of here," Jair said, walking down the stairs with her. "Can't believe all this smoke. I about fell over when I went to the bathroom and found it on fire."

"You discovered the fire?" Nina asked. "What happened?"

"Hey, Nina, move it!" Chance Ruffin said rudely, pushing past her.

"Can I talk to you later?" Nina asked Jair as she moved down the stairs.

"I'll see you outside," Jair yelled over the heads of the other students.

Nina and Keisha walked outside and found their class.

"There you are," Mrs. Maher said. "Okay, everyone's present. No talking. And stay with the class, please."

The teacher walked over to Mrs. Dominguez, the principal's secretary, to turn in her attendance list. As soon as she did, Nina and Keisha left the group. They joined Joss White, Eva Morales, and Neecy Bethune.

A light drizzle was falling. "Of course the day there's an actual fire, it rains," Eva Morales said, pulling her hoodie up over her head. "We're going to be out here forever."

In the distance, they could hear sirens.

"Hey, this is crazy, right?" Jair said, joining the group of girls.

"So tell me," Nina said, pulling out her notebook. "Give me the details. What did you see? Do you know who set it? Everything."

"This gonna be on the test?" Jair joked.

"I'm writing an article on all the stuff that's been happening," Nina said. She hadn't even thought about writing an article until the fire alarm rang. "Stolen phones and wallets, false fire alarms, and now a real fire. I don't know if it's all related. Or just lots of people doing a lot of bad stuff."

"You gonna describe me as the handsome hero of the story?" Jair asked with a smile.

"You'll always be my hero," Keisha said, kissing him on the forehead.

Keisha was president of the student government association. She had been at a party a few months back that had quickly turned rowdy. Word had spread on social media. Soon the house had been overrun with partiers. She had been surrounded by some guys who were trying to force her to drink. Jair and Zander Peterson, who was now her boyfriend, helped her escape.

Nina rolled her eyes. "Please," she said, dragging out the word. "So what happened?" she asked impatiently.

"No big deal," Jair said modestly. "I had to go, you know? So I went to the second floor boys' restroom. Some guys walked out as I went in. The trash bin was on fire. I told Doctor Miller. She hit the alarm. And here we are."

"Who were the guys walking out?" Nina asked him curiously.

"I didn't really pay attention, except for—"

Just then, the doors to the school opened. Two figures dressed in black walked out.

"I was just about to say, except for Kaleb Black. And there he is!"

"Really?" Joss said, looking concerned. "You need to tell someone."

They all looked across the parking lot. Kaleb Black and Bellamy Knight stood apart from the rest of the students. They both held notebooks. They were staring intently at the other kids.

"I wonder where the 'Black Knights' were hiding up till now?" Keisha asked, making quote marks with her fingers. "Shouldn't they have been out here with everyone else?"

Nina checked the time on her cell phone and wrote a note in her notebook. "Weird that they took so long to get out of the school," she agreed.

"You want to know who's doing stuff around here?" Jair said, watching the two dark figures. "I'd keep my eye on them."

Eva shivered. "They scare me," she said. "Ever since they started calling themselves the Black Knights, they've gotten stranger and stranger. Have you noticed how they are always watching everyone and writing in their little notebooks? It's like they're taking notes on all of us. I see them in the cafeteria, watching and writing away. What do you think they're up to?"

"I'd love to see one of their notebooks someday," Nina said. "Who knows what they've got written in there."

"Or what they're planning," Jair said darkly.

"They just look so ... threatening," Joss said, struggling to find the words. "I mean, wearing black is one thing. But ever since Bellamy hacked off her hair, she's just a hot mess."

"And that cape Kaleb wears? And those boots? The chains actually clank when he walks," Keisha added.

"You guys looking at the BKs?" Zander Peterson asked, walking up to the group. He put his arm around Keisha and kissed her.

As if he had heard Zander, Kaleb Black looked their way. He was scowling. He said something to Bellamy Knight and pointed.

Bellamy ran her fingers through what was left of her jet-black hair. It stood straight up on her head in some places. Other sections were cut so close she was almost bald. She looked directly at Jair. She nodded at something Kaleb said and wrote in her notebook.

"Well, that was freaky," Jair said nervously. "Am I on their list or something?"

"It's like they knew we were talking about them," Joss said with a shiver.

"If I had to pick two people who had something to do with this fire ..." Keisha said.

"Something's going on around here lately," Jair said. "Something not good."

Nina made a few more notes in her notebook.

"I agree," she said. "And I'd sure like to figure out who's behind it."

They all turned again to look at Kaleb and Bellamy.

"You're looking at them," Jair said.

CHAPTER 2

JAIR

Hero. It was Jair's secret name for himself.

He'd gotten his first taste of being admired a few months back when he and Zander had helped Keisha at Janelle Minnerly's party. They had also rescued Janelle when some guys dragged her into a bedroom.

The party had taken place on the same night Jair had finally stood up to his father. He'd told him to quit beating up on his brothers and his mother.

That night, he felt like a superhero. After a lifetime of feeling afraid, he felt proud of something he had done for someone else.

The feeling faded fast.

At first things were great. Life at home was much more peaceful since his father moved out.

But his mother struggled financially. Jair knew she missed his father despite the way he had treated her.

Cap Central kids were friendlier too. Jair no longer felt he had to prove himself with his fists. But he still wasn't invited to hang out with any of them. They didn't dislike him. They just never thought of him.

Jair went to the weight room at the high school a few times. He tried working out with Zander Peterson. But he was very conscious of how short and skinny he was compared to the well-built athletes who hung out there. He quit going, and then felt awkward whenever he ran into Zander.

He tried to hang out with Luther Ransome, Chance Ruffin, Thomas Porter, and the rest of his old crew. But they didn't completely trust him anymore. They had seen him too often with Zander, Keisha, and that crowd.

His old life hadn't been happy, but at least it was familiar. Jair no longer felt comfortable with his old friends, but the people he would like to be friends with never gave him a thought. He felt like he didn't fit in anywhere.

Looking back, Jair could remember one bright moment.

The night everyone thought he was a hero.

He would do anything to feel like that again.

Anything.

He started out small. When he found things in the hall, like books or clothes, he turned them in to the main office. He liked hearing Mrs. Dominguez thank him.

But he didn't care about Mrs. Dominguez. He needed Cap Central kids to look up to him.

One day in the library, he saw his chance. Nina Ambrose was checking her phone for texts. Then she laid it down on a table. Jair made sure no one was looking and pocketed the phone. Later that afternoon, he turned it in to the office. Jair had heard that Nina was thrilled when she learned someone had "found" her phone.

He started watching for opportunities. He was amazed at how careless his fellow students were. Leaving wallets in unlocked lockers, phones in gym bags, even car keys out where he could steal them easily.

He became very adept at swiping things without anyone seeing him. Then he would somehow "solve" the crimes. He would find a phone or turn in a lost wallet—a wallet he had stolen earlier. The school secretaries teased him about being the Cap Central High detective. He enjoyed their praise, but it wasn't what he was looking for.

But these acts weren't public enough. He wanted Cap Cent kids to know. What he wanted—what he *needed*—was a disaster, a potential tragedy. He wanted to swoop in, save the day, and once again hear everyone say how lucky they were that he had been there.

He wanted to be called a hero.

When he went to the boys' restroom one day and saw a smoldering cigarette on the floor, he had an idea. He picked up the cigarette and used it to try to set paper towels on fire. But they just smoldered. He used his lighter to try to start a fire in the trash bin, but the dampness snuffed out the flames.

That weekend, Jair's uncle had asked his family over for a barbeque. Jarrold was a police officer in the Metropolitan Police Department. He hadn't hung around the family much when Jair's father lived with them. Lately, he was around more. He was even teaching Jair how to drive.

As Jair helped his uncle with the grill, he got an idea.

Charcoal lighter fluid.

It made the coals light up almost instantly.

Later, he went to the Kwik n'Carry, a small convenience store on Benning Road. The first two times he stopped in, a Cap Central classmate was working behind the counter. Each time he just bought a bottle of Coke and left. He didn't want Marley Macomb there when he made his true purchase.

The third time, someone else was working. Jair bought a container of lighter fluid and several packages of notebook paper. When he got home, he poured some of the lighter fluid into an empty Coke bottle and hid it in his room.

He waited.

Observed.

Perfected his plan.

He looked around, noting where the security cameras were placed. He realized one of the school's fire alarm boxes was in a hallway far from a camera. He wore a hoodie to school one day, pulled it up over his head, and slipped out of class. He pulled the alarm. As the students streamed out of the building, he joined his class, undetected. He enjoyed listening to kids wondering who had set off the alarm.

He did it again two days later.

This time, some students sounded concerned. Now he was ready to execute his plan, but he wanted to make sure no one suspected him.

One afternoon, he saw Kaleb Black come out of a restroom. That gave Jair an idea. Kaleb Black was the perfect suspect. He wasn't like other Cap Cent students. He looked intimidating. He dressed differently. When he wasn't with the equally peculiar Bellamy Knight, he kept to himself. Jair could spread a rumor that Kaleb had started the fire. Everyone would believe him. The focus would be on Kaleb, not on Jair.

The next morning, Jair carefully packed his backpack. Books, lunch, the notebook paper, a baseball cap, and a black hoodie. He checked the cap on the Coke bottle full of lighter fluid to make sure it was on tight. Then he put the bottle in a plastic bag to protect against spills. He put it carefully in the backpack.

When the bell rang before sixth period, he raced to his locker. He put on the baseball cap to make himself taller, pulled on the hoodie, and grabbed the notebook paper and the Coke bottle. He joined the crowd of students in the hall, keeping his head down and away from the cameras. He saw the usual group of guys go into the restroom, and he slipped in among them.

He went into a stall and pulled out the package of paper. He soaked the pages in lighter fluid. When he was sure no one was in the restroom, he came out and put the paper in the trash bin. He used his lighter to set it on fire.

It caught with a *whoosh*. The flames flared high and hot, forcing him to step back. He pulled paper towels out of the dispenser and threw them on top. Then he took a deep breath. He knew the next few minutes would be crucial.

He pulled his hoodie over his face to hide from the cameras. He heard voices in the hall and opened the door a crack. A class of students was passing the door, probably heading to the computer lab. He slipped out and walked with them. He kept his head down so his face didn't show. When the class got to Dr. Miller's room, he stepped out of the line.

Dr. Miller's classroom door was open. She was helping students with their dissections on the other side of the room.

Jair pulled off his hat and hoodie and walked over to her, holding his stomach. "I don't feel well," he said. "Can I go to the bathroom?"

Dr. Miller nodded distractedly.

Jair walked down the hall. This time, he made sure he could be seen by the cameras. He walked into the boys' restroom. The fire was blazing. He got ready. Keeping from getting caught would depend on how convincing he could be.

He ran back to Dr. Miller's class and shouted that there was a fire in the restroom. Dr. Miller ran into the hall to look. Smoke was billowing out from under the door. Dr. Miller pulled the fire alarm and the school emptied.

His plan worked.

Eva Morales called him a superhero.

Joss White chatted with him like he was part of her crowd.

Exactly what he had hoped for.

Jair looked across the parking lot. He saw Kaleb and Bellamy sitting on a wall. It was almost like they wanted people to suspect them. Calling themselves the Black Knights. A play on their names, but also the image they wanted to portray. Dressing only in black. And Bellamy's goth makeup. Except for her mouth with its slash of scarlet lipstick. And Kaleb with his shaved head and piercings.

When he heard Keisha, Zander, Nina, and the others talking about the BKs, Jair knew his plan was working. Cap Central kids were already scared of Bellamy and Kaleb. It wouldn't take much to make people suspect they were responsible for the fire. He could make the whole school blame them. He'd be the only one who knew they were innocent.

CHAPTER 3

NINA

Capital Central students, attention please!" Mrs. Hess said through the bullhorn. She was standing in front of the school. Mr. Gable, the school's head of security, stood on her left. A fire department officer stood on her right. "The fire department has just informed me that we will not be able to return to the building until they complete their inspection. So I am going to have to dismiss you now. You will not be able to return to the building to claim your things until tomorrow."

The students groaned.

"What about our phones?" someone yelled.

"I need my car keys!" a boy called out.

"Does this mean no homework?" Zander asked.

Students cheered.

Mrs. Hess put up her hand. "If you need your book bags for homework, then yes, this means no homework," she said. "Although most of your assignments are posted online, so you can keep up at home. Teachers, I'm instructing you to be lenient tomorrow regarding due dates. As for phones, you'll just have to live without them for a night. Car keys do present a problem. Anyone whose keys are in the building, please come see me."

Nina said goodbye to her friends. She walked over to Mrs. Hess, Mr. Gable, and the fire department officer. Melinda Stevens, another student, was talking to Mr. Gable.

"I'm Nina Ambrose. I'm a reporter on the Cap Central *Star*," Nina said to the fire department officer. "May I ask you some questions?"

"You can ask," the fire department officer said. "But I'll only answer what I can."

"Can you tell me your name and title?" Nina said, ready to write in her notebook.

"I'm Battalion Chief Demetrius Wilhelm. How can I help you?"

"Do you believe this fire was deliberately set?" Nina asked.

"We aren't done with our investigation, but that's certainly a possibility," Chief Wilhelm answered.

Nina turned to Mrs. Hess and Mr. Gable. "Is it your feeling—either of you—that there have been more ..." She struggled for the right word. "Well, incidents at Cap Cent lately? Items stolen? Stuff like that?"

"You know, Nina, there are always going to be some students who don't respect others," Mrs. Hess said. "We at Cap Central try to emphasize a culture of respect and—"

"Mrs. Hess, come on!" Nina interrupted impatiently. "Something's up, don't you think? Seems like every day something is stolen. Those false alarms last week. And now somebody sets the school on fire? Are you investigating this as some sort of crime spree? Maybe something that could lead to even bigger crimes?"

"Do you know anything you could share with us?" Mr. Gable asked. "Do you have any suspicions?"

"You think it's related?" Nina asked, writing in her notebook.

"I didn't say that, but we'll consider every possibility in our investigation," Mr. Gable said. "Now, anything you can share with us?"

Nina thought about Bellamy and Kaleb. How they had acted. She didn't want to make a false accusation, but like everyone else, she wanted an end to the recent crimes.

"I don't know anything specific," she said. "But you might want to look at the security tapes after the fire alarm rang. There were some students who came outside much later than everyone else."

"You could save us some time if you'd tell us who you mean," the fire chief said. "We will keep the information confidential. But there are lots of cameras, and it will take us a long time to go through the tapes."

Nina was quiet for a minute. "I want to write about this for the *Star*," she said. "If I help you with your investigation, can you help me by answering questions when I'm writing my piece for the school paper?"

Chief Wilhelm took out a business card.

He took out a pen and wrote something on the back of the card. "Here's my business card. On the front is my office phone number and email address. I just wrote my personal cell number on the back. You call me anytime for information, and I'll tell you what I know. I can't share anything that could hurt our investigation, but besides that, I'll always talk to you."

Nina took the card and put it in her pocket. She looked at Melinda. She didn't want to talk in front of another student.

Mr. Gable saw her look. "Melinda volunteers with the police department," he said. "She's joining the academy as soon as she graduates so she can become a police officer. She knows anything she hears must be kept confidential. Right?" he said, addressing Melinda.

"Right," Melinda agreed. "I'd blow my chances to be a cadet if I told anything I heard in an investigation."

"Okay," Nina said. "You should look for the BKs. Bellamy Knight and Kaleb Black."

"They dress in all black and call themselves 'the Black Knights,' like they're comic book characters," Melinda said to Chief Wilhelm.

"I'll keep my eye on them," Mr. Gable told Chief Wilhelm. "That's them, sitting over on that wall." He nodded in their direction.

They all turned to look at Bellamy and Kaleb. The two students were reading something in a notebook Kaleb was holding.

"What makes you think they had something to do with the fire?" Chief Wilhelm asked, turning back to Nina.

"They came out later than everyone else. Much later," Nina answered. "And Jair said Kaleb was near the boys' restroom right before he discovered the fire."

"Jair? Jair Nobles?" Mr. Gable asked. "He said he discovered the fire?"

Nina nodded.

"Guess we'd better talk to this Jair," Chief Wilhelm said. "Can you find him for us?" he asked Mrs. Hess.

The fire chief turned back to Nina. "You've been really helpful," he said. "I'd better get back to the cleanup. But remember, call me anytime. And good luck with your article."

Nina closed her notebook. Lots of students remained in the parking lot, though many had left. She looked around for her friends. But she couldn't find anyone. She put her notebook in her back pocket and started for home.

So far her assignments for the online newspaper had been about Cap Central's new pom-pom squad, proposed changes in the bell schedule, and how the uneven heat in the building made some rooms too hot, while others were too cold.

She wanted to find something to write about that would make a difference. The kind of story people would talk about over lunch. A crime spree at the school that included arson was exactly the kind of story she'd been looking for.

CHAPTER 4

JAIR

Jair watched Nina and Melinda Stevens talk to Mr. Gable, Mrs. Hess, and someone from the fire department. He was jealous. He had discovered the fire. He should be the one they were turning to for information.

He was just about to leave when he saw Mrs. Hess beckon to him. He walked past the groups of students still standing around. He tried to look nonchalant, but inside he was excited. He figured Nina had told them he had discovered the fire. He imagined how grateful they were going to be.

"Jair, this is Battalion Chief Wilhelm," Mr. Gable said. "We need to talk to you about what you saw. You got a minute?"

"Sure," Jair said. He stuck out his hand toward Chief Wilhelm. As the chief shook his hand, Jair could see other students looking at him as they left the school grounds. He felt pretty important shaking hands with a fire chief.

"I understand you're the guy who discovered the fire," Chief Wilhelm said.

Jair nodded. "It was burning when I went into the boys' restroom. I came out and told Doctor Miller. She pulled the alarm."

The fire chief nodded. "Good thing for the school you were there," he said. "Sounds like the right person, in the right place. And at the right time."

Jair beamed. The chief's words were just what he wanted to hear. He wished Nina could have heard them and written them down for her article.

"So it was in the trash bin?" Chief Wilhelm asked.

"Yeah," Jair said. "Burning out of control."

The chief nodded knowingly. "Odd, though," he said. "Usually restroom trash bins are full of damp paper towels. Can't get them to ignite no matter what you do."

Something about his tone made Jair's heart skip a beat. He glanced at Mr. Gable and saw that the security officer was looking at him seriously. He was not smiling.

Jair shrugged. "I don't know about that," he said, trying to sound nonchalant. "I just know what I saw."

"Son, who else was in the restroom when you got there?" Mr. Gable asked.

Jair was prepared for this question. "I knew you were going to ask me that," he said with a laugh. "I really didn't pay attention," he said. "I only saw one person, but I don't want to make any false accusations."

"Why don't you tell us who you saw, and we'll look at the tapes ourselves?" Mr. Gable said.

Jair looked at Melinda.

"You can speak freely in front of Melinda," Mr. Gable said. "She volunteers with the police department and wants to join the academy when she graduates. She knows to keep anything she hears confidential."

Melinda nodded.

Jair turned back to the officials. "Well, don't tell anybody I was the one who told you. But

Kaleb Black was coming out of the boys' restroom when I went in," Jair said.

Mr. Gable and Chief Wilhelm exchanged a funny look.

"Did you notice anything else?" Mr. Gable asked. "Did he look nervous? Was he running?"

Jair shrugged. "He looked like he always does," he said. "You know what I mean. All goth and stuff."

"Son, we may need to talk to you again, okay?" Chief Wilhelm said. "After we look at the tape and all. You might want to tell your parents, in case they'd like to be present."

Jair was starting to feel very scared. "Why would my parents want to be there?" he asked.

"Arson is a felony," Mr. Gable said. "And from the looks of things, whoever did this planned it carefully. That makes it an even more serious crime. Whoever is responsible will be expelled and probably charged. We'll conduct a formal investigation, and you're going to have to make a statement."

"Do I need a lawyer?" Jair asked shakily. He hated how nervous his voice sounded.

"I don't know. Do you think you need a

lawyer?" Chief Wilhelm asked. His voice was hard and serious.

"Nah, just asking," Jair said. "My uncle's a police officer. Maybe I'll bring him. Anyway, it's cool. Call me anytime."

"Who's your uncle?" Mr. Gable asked.

"Jarrold Norris," Jair said.

"I know Jarrold. I'll fill him in when I see him," Mr. Gable said. "Thanks again for your help, Jair."

Jair turned to leave. He felt scared. The great feeling he'd had earlier was completely gone. Instead of feeling like a hero, he felt like a criminal.

CHAPTER 5

NINA

Are you kidding me?" Joss White's voice rang out down the hallway.

Nina Ambrose turned to see what caused her outburst.

Joss was standing in front of her locker. The door was ajar. Books and other items spilled out onto the floor.

Nina walked over and looked at the mess. "What's up?" she asked.

Joss opened her backpack. "I can't find my phone anywhere," she said. "It was in the outside pocket of my pack. I always keep it there during school. The pocket is zipped. Always. Now the phone is gone."

"Was your backpack in your locker all day?" Nina asked.

"Yeah, except when—oh no!" Joss said, hitting her forehead. "I left it on a table in the cafeteria at breakfast this morning, for like five seconds," she said. "I got up to throw my stuff away and stopped to talk to Neecy Bethune and Charlie Ray. I didn't check for my phone after that, but I'll bet that's when it got stolen. Why can't they catch this guy?"

Nina shook her head in disgust. "There are so many kids getting jacked lately," she said. "Whoever it is, he's really good at this. In and out before anyone notices."

Joss shook her head in disgust. "Honestly, if I knew who it was," she said. "Now what am I going to do? I'm not due for a new phone for a year. I can't afford to buy another one now."

"Why don't you just suspend the service for a day or two?" Nina asked. "In case it turns up."

"As if it's going to," Joss said bitterly.

"Mine did, remember?" Nina said. "Last month. I lost my phone and thought I had to buy a new one. But I kept checking the office. A few days later someone turned it in." She shook her head. "It still bothers me. I know I didn't just leave it somewhere. I'm really careful. Someone stole it, but then left it where somebody honest found it."

"That's crazy," Joss said. "Whoever's doing this stuff, he's getting bolder."

"Or she, for that matter," Nina said. "It could be a girl, you know. You gonna tell security?"

"Yeah. I'll check in with Ms. Phelan, and then go down to see Mister Gable," Joss said. "This really makes me mad." She slammed her locker door in anger.

Nina shook her head in sympathy. "Maybe whoever's doing this will mess up, then we'll find out who it is."

"Well, whoever it is, I hope they lock him up. With my luck, I probably chose a table nowhere near one of the security cameras," Joss said. "Mister Gable probably won't be able to see anything on the tape."

The two girls walked down the hall. When they got to Ms. Phelan's chemistry class, Nina took her seat. After asking Ms. Phelan for permission to go talk to security, Joss left.

Nina sat at her desk and pulled out her notebook. She scribbled some notes about the theft. Where Joss's locker was located. The time of day the theft was discovered. And every other detail she could remember.

She had asked Mr. Gable for a list of all the thefts that had been reported since the beginning of the school year. She wanted to see if there was a pattern.

Ms. Phelan had just started the lesson when the door opened and Joss walked back in. She was grinning as she took her seat. "Found it," she said happily, showing Nina her phone. "You're not going to believe this. Jair found it and turned it in to the main office."

Nina shook her head in amazement. "Jair, again?" she said. "He's on a roll lately."

When the lunch bell rang, Nina grabbed her notebook as well as her lunch. She headed for the cafeteria and looked for her friends. She found them at their usual table. She squeezed into an empty seat between Marcus DiMonte and Lionel "Ferg" Ferguson. Ferg was hefty and took up a lot of room.

Soon Eva Morales, Carlos Garcia, and Joss joined them. Joss was still smiling.

"I guess you're having a good day," Nina said with a smile.

"Yeah, I've gotta find Jair to thank him," Joss said. "He just saved me some major money."

"He probably didn't even know the phone was yours," Eva said. "He'll be glad when he hears."

"Oh! There he is," Joss said. She put her lunch on the table and walked over to Jair. She said something to him, and he grinned. Then she gave him a hug and kissed him on the cheek. She started to walk away. But then she turned back to him to say something.

Jair looked over to where Nina and the others were watching. He gave a little wave and said something to Joss, shaking his head.

Joss walked back over and sat down.

"So?" Eva said. "What'd he say?"

"He found it in the boys' restroom. Can you believe it?" Joss said, taking out her lunch. "Somebody apparently stole the phone and then left it there. Gross!"

"What a genius," Carlos said. "I'm just glad you got it back."

"I'm going to go talk to Jair before class," Nina said, grabbing her lunch tray. "See you guys later."

She threw out her trash and headed for the cafeteria doors. She nearly bumped into Kaleb Black and Bellamy Knight as they walked in. She had never been this close to them before. Bellamy's makeup was very dramatic, and Nina had a hard time not staring.

"See something interesting?" Bellamy asked in a sarcastic tone.

Nina stopped. She had an idea. "Actually, I sort of find the two of you interesting," she said. "I'm on the school paper, and I'm always trying to find new things to write about. Could I interview you both some day?"

Bellamy and Kaleb looked at each other. Kaleb shrugged.

"Why?" Bellamy asked.

"Wait—yes! Yes, of course," Kaleb answered enthusiastically. He looked meaningfully at Bellamy. "Right?"

"Good idea," Bellamy said. "Hadn't thought of that."

Nina looked from one to the other. Bellamy

and Kaleb were having a conversation in front of her, but she could not understand what they were talking about.

"So is that a yes? I'm Nina, by the way," Nina said.

"He's Kaleb," Bellamy said.

"She's Bellamy," Kaleb said.

They looked at each other. "We're the Black Knights" they said in unison.

Nina thought they were the strangest students she'd ever spoken to. "About that interview," she said again.

"Name the time," Bellamy said.

"Name the *place*," Kaleb added.

"You need more makeup," Bellamy said.

"On your *face*," Kaleb finished.

Nina was silent. She realized her mouth was open in surprise. She shut it and said, "Okay. Thanks for the tip. I'll check that out. Meanwhile, I'm working on something else right now, but I'll talk to you soon, okay?"

"She'll talk to us *soon*," Bellamy said.

"Has to be after *noon*," Kaleb said.

"But not when there's a full *moon*," Bellamy added.

They talk like cartoon characters, Nina thought as she watched them walk out of the cafeteria. She laughed to herself. Now that she had seen and talked to them up close, they seemed more unusual than threatening. She was actually looking forward to interviewing them.

But first she wanted to follow up on the idea of the recent crimes being connected. Jair was in her sixth period health class. She hoped she could have a few minutes to talk to him before class started.

She climbed the stairs to the third floor. Jair stood at the top of the stairs with Thomas Porter, Luther Ransome, and Chance Ruffin. She walked toward where they were standing. As she approached, they all quit talking and just looked at her.

"What's up?" Jair said.

Nina didn't feel comfortable around the other boys. She wasn't going to talk to Jair in front of them.

"Could I talk to you for a minute?" she asked.

Jair turned and said something to his friends that she couldn't catch. They all laughed.

"Later, homes," Luther said, giving Jair a fist bump. The three boys walked away, leaving Nina alone with Jair.

"What was that about?" Nina asked.

"Nothing," Jair said. "What did you want to ask me?"

Nina took out her notebook. "I heard you found Joss's phone. Like I told you after the fire, I'm writing an article about all the incidents that have been happening here lately. Stolen phones, fire alarms, the fire, whatever. I wondered what you could tell me about where you found Joss's phone."

"Not much to tell," Jair said. "I went into the boys' restroom. It was on a shelf above the sink. Like someone forgot it. I turned it in to Mrs. Dominguez. It wasn't until lunch that I learned it was Joss's."

"So how did it get into the boys' restroom?" Nina asked.

"How would I know?" Jair answered. "I didn't leave it there. I just found it."

"Right," Nina said. "But why do you think someone stole Joss's phone and then left it there?"

"Who knows?" Jair said. "Probably just forgot he had it."

"It's odd," Nina said. "Because the same thing happened to me. My phone disappeared, and then someone turned it in to the office."

"Where did you leave it?" Jair asked.

"I didn't leave it anywhere. It went missing from my backpack. I think someone took it."

"When was this?" Jair asked.

"Last month."

"What did it look like?"

"Well, here it is," Nina said, pulling her phone out of her pocket.

"Oh! I found that phone too," Jair said. "Had no idea it was yours. Found it in the boys' restroom. The one by the trophy case."

"You're kidding," Nina said. "*You* found my phone? *And* Joss's phone?"

"Crazy, right?" Jair said, shaking his head. "Just glad I was able to help you girls out." He gave a little laugh.

Nina was quiet for a moment. Something just didn't feel right about what Jair was saying. Finding a stolen phone was unusual. Finding two was more than unusual. It was crazy lucky.

And to learn that both phones had been owned by his friends?

Nina knew if it were her, she'd be pretty freaked out by the coincidence. But Jair didn't seem impressed by the odds. He sounded matter of fact, like it was something that happened every day.

"Weird," Nina said, writing in her notebook. "Ever find anything besides the two phones?"

"Oh, you know. Stuff here and there," he said vaguely.

"Yeah?" Nina pressed. "Like what?"

"Hey, Ms. B.'s gonna be here soon," Jair said, looking over Nina's shoulder. "Talk to you later."

Nina turned. Ms. Billingsley was nowhere in sight.

"Wait. Just tell me this. How does it feel to turn stuff in? Or discover a fire?" Nina asked. "Nothing like that ever happens to me, so I really want to know."

Nina suspected Jair would talk a little more freely about his discoveries if he thought Nina was a little envious.

"It's no big deal," Jair said, sounding modest and boastful at the same time. He started to walk away. "Right place, right time. Anybody would do the same. I'm just happy to help."

"Jair, hold up!" Nina said. "Do you have any suspicions about who is stealing the phones? And why he—since it seems to be a boy—is just leaving them around?"

"No clue," Jair said, shaking his head. "Although …"

"Although?" Nina prompted.

"Nothing. I don't want to accuse anybody. But whoever it is? I wish they'd catch him. Not right to take something that's not yours."

"Right," Nina agreed. "Even if the person eventually gets it back. It's just wrong."

The last part came out more forcefully than she had meant it to. She closed up her notebook.

"Can I go now?" Jair asked.

"Yeah, thanks," Nina answered.

"Not a problem," Jair said.

Ms. Billingsley walked up and unlocked her door. The class took their seats.

"Anybody save a life this weekend?" Ms. Billingsley asked.

No one answered. She put her hands on her hips. "Class, I told you I'd reward you if you ever actually got to use what I've been teaching you in our first aid unit," she said. "Now, please, start finding some victims, okay?"

"Oh, now I remember. I used it," Jair said, raising his hand.

The class laughed.

"And as I said before, as long as it's verified, of course," Ms. Billingsley said good-naturedly. "Now, today we're going to learn what to do if someone is choking."

Nina looked over the notes she had written about the thefts. The same person recovered two stolen cell phones. And both phones owned by his friends? An amazing stroke of luck. And then discovering a fire?

Too much of a coincidence.

She didn't believe in coincidences.

CHAPTER 6

JAIR

Jair was concerned about his conversation with Nina. She was asking too many questions. He knew she was trying to write an article for the school's online newspaper, but her tone made him wary.

When Jair got home after school, he found his uncle Jarrold sitting in the kitchen. He was talking to his sister, Jair's mother. Since Jair's father had left, Jarrold had been spending more time at the Nobleses' apartment, playing with the little kids, and sometimes showing up with a take-out dinner. He usually came straight from work, wearing his uniform, his gun on his belt.

Best of all, he'd taught Jair how to drive. He'd taken Jair out for driving practice at least once a week. D.C. law required forty hours of driving before kids could get their licenses. Jair's mother didn't have a car, so Uncle Jarrold was the only way Jair was going to learn to drive.

Jair waited impatiently as Uncle Jarrold played a game of slapjack with his two little brothers. Several times Uncle Jarrold asked Jair to join them, but he refused. Finally his mother told the boys to get ready for bed.

Uncle Jarrold kissed them both, and then tossed his car keys to Jair. "Ready to roll?" he asked his nephew.

Jair nodded happily. "Where do you want to go? I need more practice."

"Don't be out too late," Jair's mother called as they headed out.

Once they settled in the car, Jarrold said, "Go to New York Avenue. Then get on the B–W Parkway. Take it to the Beltway. You need more practice with highway driving."

Jair started the car. He did everything Jarrold had told him. He slowly drove onto New York Avenue. He took the exit for the Baltimore–Washington Parkway and merged into traffic. He was concentrating so hard. He wasn't talking. He barely breathed.

Once he got on the Beltway, he relaxed a bit. There wasn't much traffic, and it was moving smoothly.

"So I heard there was some excitement at Cap Central a few days ago," Jarrold said.

"What do you mean?" Jair asked.

"One of my guys said you discovered a fire," Jarrold said.

"Yeah, it was crazy," Jair said. "Walked into the boys' restroom and found it blazing."

"Fire in a school," Jarrold said, shaking his head. "Everybody get out okay?"

"Yeah, I think they put it out pretty quickly," Jair said. "Guess I discovered it in time."

"Good thing," Jarrold said. "That could have been bad."

Jair was thrilled. Now even his uncle was praising him.

"Hey, you know a girl named Melinda Stevens?" Jarrold asked.

"Yeah, she goes to Cap Cent. Why?"

"I see her around the station house," Jarrold said. "I heard she's joining the cadets as soon as she graduates. Seems pretty eager. She goes on ride-alongs a lot."

"Ride-alongs?" Jair repeated. "What are those?"

"When civilians ride in police cars with the officers," Jarrold said. "A lot of people do it. You have to stay in the car if something goes down, but it can be pretty interesting. Or boring, actually, depending on what's happening. You interested?"

"Yeah," Jair said. "Sounds pretty cool."

"We'll get you signed up," Jarrold said. "Now, why don't you get off at the next exit. You can get back on the Beltway going in the other direction. Then get back on the B–W Parkway and go back into town."

Jair was quiet as he concentrated. Before too long, he was back in front of his apartment.

"You're doing real well," Jarrold said. "How many more hours do you need before you can take your test?"

"Eighteen," Jair answered.

"Won't be long," Jarrold said. "Anyway, I'm off. Tell your mom and those little boys I said good night."

"Hey, thanks, Uncle Jarrold," Jair said.

"For?" Jarrold asked.

"Letting me practice driving in your car."

"You kidding? Least I can do to pay you guys back."

"Pay us back?" Jair said. "For what?"

"For letting me hang here," Jarrold said. "You and your brothers make me feel real good. My sister can't cook, but I like hanging with my family."

Jair laughed. "I'm telling my mom you said that," he said.

"You do, and that's the last time you use my car," Jarrold said. "See you later, son,"

Jair beamed. He went inside with a smile.

CHAPTER 7

NINA

Nina sat down to do her homework. Tomorrow was the first class period of the month. In journalism class story ideas were due.

Ms. Cooper, the journalism teacher, had a strict rule. Each reporter was required to turn in a list of at least three possible article ideas at the beginning of every month. The editors would read the descriptions and assign the articles. Since school began, Nina never failed to come up with three ideas.

She wasn't ready to share her ideas with the editors yet, which meant she had nothing to turn in. She wanted to break the story of who was committing the recent crimes at the school. The story would take a huge amount of investigative work. She knew she might not ever be able to prove who was behind the crimes.

The easy way out would be to simply report that there had been an increase in thefts at the school. She would tie in the false fire alarms and the actual fire. She knew she could get comments from Mr. Gable, Chief Wilhelm, and Mrs. Hess. But she wanted more.

Her other idea was to write about Bellamy and Kaleb. She was curious about why they called themselves the Black Knights, why they dressed so dramatically, and what they wrote when they scribbled in their notebooks. They looked so suspicious. She almost hoped she could discover some horrible event they were planning. And prevent it from happening.

Either story would be a total triumph. But she had no real proof that any one person was behind the recent crimes. She didn't even know if there had been more of those incidents lately than usual. And she had absolutely no proof that Bellamy and Kaleb were planning anything.

She took out the outline sheet with her story ideas. The sheet listed the five Ws: who, what, when, where, why. She thought about the

Bellamy and Kaleb article. The only blank she could fill in was the "who." She had nothing more.

> *Two kids who dressed differently.*
> *Who other students seemed scared of.*

Not enough to turn in to her editors.

She started a new five-Ws sheet for the crime story. In the space for "what" she listed the crimes she knew about: the false fire alarms, the actual fire, Marcus DiMonte's stolen wallet, and her and Joss's stolen phones. The list wasn't as long as she had thought. If this were an actual crime spree, she needed more.

She turned on her computer and accessed the *Cap Cent Convo*, a blog started recently after another blog had to be taken down when it targeted an autistic student at the school.

She posted a question to the site, asking if anyone had been the victim of a crime at school, particularly thefts of phones, wallets, or other small items.

Within a couple of hours, she had heard from lots of students. Some of the stories were cases where they simply lost their phones, purses, or wallets. She rejected those. But in other cases, the students knew their items had been stolen. They knew approximately when they had last seen the item, how the thief had gotten access, and when they had discovered the loss. The odd thing, though, was how many of the items ended up being returned.

Nina made a note to call other D.C. schools to check out how often phones were lost and then found.

She knew she still didn't have enough information to tie together the lost items and the fire. But even the lost items issue could be the basis for a decent article. She pulled out the five-Ws sheet and filled out what she knew.

WHO: ?

WHAT: *Number of stolen phones, purses, and wallets. Number returned. Do Cap Cent kids get stuff back more than other high schools? If so, what is going on?*

WHEN: *When did thefts begin?*

WHERE: *Duh. School.*

WHY: ?

Right before going to bed, Nina accessed her email one last time. She had a message from a senior she didn't know. The girl told what seemed to be the usual story. She had set her backpack down for a minute, got distracted, picked it back up and realized later that her phone was missing. But this story ended differently.

When Mrs. Dominguez called me down to say that my phone had been turned in, I was so happy. I wanted to do something for the nice person who was so honest. I learned that his name was Jair Nobles. I don't know him. Do you?

Jair. Again.

Jair had talked about finding her and Joss's phones. But he never said anything about the same thing happening with any other phones.

The more Nina thought about it, the more she was convinced. Jair was both the bad guy and the good guy. Stealing phones and then turning them in. Maybe even starting the fire and then discovering it. She didn't know why he would do these things.

She also didn't know how far he'd go.

CHAPTER 8

JAIR

Jair saw Nina's question on the blog. He wondered how many responses she would get. He thought back over the past several months and tried to remember how many times he had turned phones, wallets, and other items in to the main office. He hoped he hadn't overdone it.

He had tried to be careful. Sometimes he had waited until Mrs. Dominguez was out of the office so he could hand in the item to another secretary. He loved hearing the secretaries tell him how honest he was. How much they knew the owner of the item would appreciate what he'd done.

He'd never thought anyone would see a pattern. Never suspect.

He needed to ramp-up suspicion toward Kaleb and Bellamy. With their peculiar style of dress and unusual behavior, they were the perfect suspects. They were different, and that made them stand out.

He had to find a way to make Nina focus on the Black Knights.

At lunch he sat at the end of his usual table with Luther Ransome, Chance Ruffin, and Thomas Porter. He didn't pay much attention to their conversation. He was focused on Nina Ambrose. She sat with Joss White and Eva Morales.

As he watched, Nina got up from the table. Jair stood. He started for the trash can. He wanted it to look as if he had just happened to arrive there at the same time as Nina.

As he crossed the cafeteria, he saw Keshawn Connor coming from the food line. Keshawn was on crutches. He had both crutches under one arm. He was trying to carry a lunch tray with his free hand. He was hopping. Nina dumped her trash and walked over to him. She said something, and he laughed and nodded. She took his tray and set it down on the table. The other students all turned to him and began talking. Keshawn laughed at something Neecy Bethune said. Nina patted Keshawn on the shoulder and started for the doors. Jair took off after her.

"Hey, Nina!" he called.

She stopped and waited.

"What's up with Keshawn?" he asked.

"Sprained his ankle helping some little old lady in his building last night," Nina said. "Tripped over one of her cats. Why?"

"Just wondering," Jair said. "I saw your post last night. Get many responses?"

"A few," she answered.

"Just wondered if you'd solved the crimes yet," Jair said with a laugh. It sounded fake, even to him.

"Not yet," Nina said. "Why? Do you have any theories?"

Just then, a security guard's voice bellowed, "Bellamy and Kaleb, you need to throw out your trash."

Nina and Jair both turned. Bellamy and Kaleb were leaving the cafeteria. They were walking quickly.

"You'd better get back here. I'm tired of your mess!" the guard yelled.

As they got near Nina and Jair, Kaleb stopped. He looked at Nina and winked humorously. Then he spun around twice and walked out. Bellamy never stopped.

"Well, that was … unusual," Jair said. "You know them?"

"Not really," Nina said as she walked out of the cafeteria. "Why?"

"It's just … I don't know. I don't want to say," Jair said.

"Say what?" Nina asked.

"Well, I just … I just don't trust them. I see Kaleb in the halls a lot, and one time I saw him trying to open a few locker doors. He saw me watching and gave me a look. I can't describe it, but it was … well, sorta scary. Evil, almost. Ever since then he acts like he has it in for me. Like I'm on his list. Now that I think about it, each time I've found a phone, Kaleb was nearby. I just wonder …"

"I don't know," Nina said skeptically. "He didn't really act odd or hostile to you just now. And why would he be stealing stuff but leaving it to be turned in? Why would someone do that?"

"Maybe to scare people?" Jair answered. "Make them think Cap Central isn't a safe place."

Nina laughed. "That doesn't make sense. Maybe it's nothing. People are always going to be careless and lose their things. Maybe it's been just a run of bad luck."

"I don't know," Jair said. "Seems like it's out of control to me. I just hope I'm wrong about the BKs. All those other places, the school shootings? People always said afterward that they thought the shooter was scary. But they didn't do anything about it. I'd hate to have that here."

Nina stopped. "You feel that strongly about it? Do something," she scolded. "Tell somebody. Tell Mister Gable. Or another security guard."

Jair could see she wasn't convinced. "I just thought if you could hint at them being behind it in your article ..." he said, his voice trailing off.

"I'm not going to 'hint' at anything without any proof," Nina said angrily. "That's not how it works. You got a problem with Bellamy and Kaleb? You deal with it. Don't try to get me to do your dirty work for you."

She walked off down the hall in a huff.

Jair watched her for a minute. Then he headed for the stairs.

The conversation hadn't gone at all well. Now Nina was angry. Being on her bad side might make her suspicious of him. He had no idea where she was going. She was in his next class.

At the top of the stairs, he turned toward Ms. Billingsley's health class. Melinda Stevens was sitting on the floor, reading a book.

Jair stood in front of her. "Hey," he said.

Melina looked up. "What?" she said.

"What are you reading?" he asked.

Melinda looked at him curiously. "*Flowers in the Attic*," she said. "Why?"

"Just wondered if it was some police book or something," Jair said. "You hanging out with cops and all."

"Hanging out with cops?" Melinda repeated in an amused voice. "What's that mean?"

"My uncle's a cop. He said you go on ride-alongs and stuff," Jair said. "And I saw you talking to Mister Gable and the fire chief the other day."

"So?" Melinda said. "Why do you care?"

"No reason," Jair said. "What are ride-alongs like?"

"Why? You want to go on one?"

"Maybe," Jair said. "You get to see anything interesting?"

"Sometimes," Melinda said. "I was in a car that chased down a guy once. That was pretty cool. Mostly I just listen to the cops as they ride around. And depending on what's going on and who I'm riding with, I get to be on the scene as they're handling stuff. It's interesting."

"You like it?" Jair asked.

"I do," Melinda answered, putting down her book. "I'm thinking of joining the academy when I graduate."

Jair sat down beside her. "So how often do you do these ride-alongs?" Jair asked.

"Oh, about every month or so," Melinda said. "You should do it. It's really fun."

"Don't know if I'd ever want to be a cop," Jair said. "Though lately, I sort of feel like one, trying to solve all these stolen phone crimes and all."

"What do you mean?" Melinda asked.

"Just that there seem to be a lot of phones and wallets getting stolen. I have my suspicions about who is doing it, but so far, no one has listened to me."

"Who do you think?" Melinda asked.

"I don't want to say, but—"

Just then, Kaleb and Bellamy entered the hallway. Kaleb dropped his books with a loud crash. "Go to the end and wait for me," he said to Bellamy. "Tell me when you're ready to film."

Bellamy walked down to the end of the hallway. "Ready," she called out, holding her phone up.

Kaleb took off running. It looked as if he was going to crash into the wall at the end of the hall. His momentum carried him part way up the wall, but then he crumpled into a heap on the floor.

Bellamy ran to him.

"Ouch," he said, picking himself up. He dusted off his clothes. "Did you get it?"

"Hope so," Bellamy said. "Maybe you need to do something different with your feet."

"I still think handsprings would be best," he said. "I just can't do them."

Jair turned back toward Melinda. "I think Mister Gable should keep an eye on them," Jair said softly. "I feel like they're planning something. Something big."

"Like what?' Melinda asked.

"I don't know. I just hope it's not something horrible," Jair said, shaking his head.

He and Melinda grew silent as Kaleb came back to where he had dropped his books. Kaleb pulled a small notebook out of his pocket. He looked at Jair and Melinda and wrote something in the notebook.

"What are you writing?" Jair called out.

Kaleb put away the notebook. "Keeping a list," he said.

"What kind of a list?" Jair asked.

"A long list," Kaleb answered. He picked up his books and walked away from Jair and Melinda. As he joined Bellamy at the other end of the hall, he said something to her. The two of them turned and looked at Melinda and Jair. Bellamy nodded. Then they walked around the corner out of sight.

"Okay, that was weird," Melinda said. "I see what you mean."

"I know, right?" Jair said. "I'm just sayin'. Glad you see it too. No one else seems to notice."

Ms. Billingsley walked up to them and unlocked her classroom door. Jair stood up and waited for Melinda. They walked into class together and took their seats.

The door opened again. Keshawn hobbled in on his crutches. Charlie Ray followed and took the crutches from him after he sat down.

"That's what you get for being a nice guy to little old ladies," Marcus DiMonte yelled from across the room.

Jair watched everyone fussing over Keshawn. He couldn't believe it. Keshawn Connor? He was a nobody. Not an athlete, not friends with Neecy or that crowd. Not anybody. But because he was on crutches, all of a sudden he was the most popular guy at Cap Central.

It gave him an idea.

CHAPTER 9

NINA

Nina didn't know what to think about Jair's accusations. On the one hand, Kaleb and Bellamy were definitely different. Their appearance was sort of scary, like characters in a Batman movie. On the other hand, Nina suspected Jair was trying to manipulate her into focusing on them. She still thought Jair was responsible for the missing phones. But she didn't know how to prove it.

Her article ideas were still due.

She got to journalism class after health. She pulled out her assignment sheets. She filled in one sheet for interviewing Bellamy and Kaleb. She was no further along in getting information about them than she had been when she first got the idea. So the amount of detail she could list to justify doing the article was light. She doubted her editors would allow her to do the assignment.

She completed another sheet about investigating whether students were cleaning up after themselves at lunch. She didn't even know if trash was a problem. But she had to come up with three ideas. She hoped the editors wouldn't choose this idea.

She then focused on the theft idea. She knew she could do a decent article about the recent incidents, the thefts and the fire alarms and fire. But she really wanted to do more. She wanted to be able to say who was responsible and why.

She explained her dilemma to Ms. Cooper, the journalism teacher. She didn't share her suspicions about who was responsible.

"You know, you can't accuse someone if he or she hasn't been charged," Ms. Cooper said. "Your role is to report what has happened, get officials to say where they are with the investigation, get reaction from the staff and students, that sort of thing. Leave the investigation to the authorities."

Nina knew she was probably right, but it

felt like only half the story. She completed the assignment sheet, though, and started making phone calls. It would be a few days before the editors would make the assignments. In the meantime, she could do some background work.

She got on the website for D.C. Public Schools. She sent emails to the principals and security guards at each, asking for statistics on false fire alarms and actual fires. She also asked about thefts of wallets and cell phones. Finally, she asked each to estimate how many of the items were actually recovered. She sent the same email to principals and security guards at a few high schools in Maryland and Virginia, just for comparison.

When the bell rang at the end of the day, Nina headed for Ms. Phelan's classroom. She needed some extra help with chemistry. After she finished, she went to her locker. Her locker was in a hallway that didn't include many class-rooms. At this hour, the hallway was deserted. She opened it and thought about the books she needed to take home.

All of a sudden, she felt like someone was

watching her. She turned around. Bellamy and Kaleb were standing silently behind her. Nina gasped and dropped her books.

"You scared me half to death," she said. She bent down to pick up her things. "Where did you come from anyway?"

Neither student said anything.

"Whatever," Nina said angrily. She slammed her locker door shut and spun the lock.

"You wanted to *talk*," Kaleb said.

"So start to *walk*," Bellamy said.

"Now?" Nina asked. She did want to talk to them. But being alone with them in the deserted school wasn't what she had in mind.

"You scared?" Kaleb said.

"No," Nina lied. "Just not prepared."

"She's got it," Bellamy said excitedly to Kaleb. "Great job," she added, turning back to Nina.

"I know, right? I told you we could trust her," Kaleb said.

Nina looked from one to the other. "I have no clue what you're talking about," she said.

"You *rhymed*," Bellamy said.

"In no *time*," Kaleb said.

"What are you talking about?" Nina asked, frustrated. "When did I rhyme? And why do you—I don't get what's going on here. Can you start at the beginning?"

" 'Cause you're not *scared*," Bellamy chanted.

"Just *unprepared*," Kaleb said in a singsong voice.

"When was the beginning *anyway*?" Bellamy said to Kaleb.

"There was no beginning, no *specific day*," Kaleb answered.

"Okay, this isn't going to work," Nina said angrily. "I don't know what your thing is, but I'm not getting it. I'd like to talk to you sometime, but not like this. If you ever want to actually talk, and not fool around with me, let me know."

"We'll talk, but not *here*," Kaleb said. "Lately this building is full of *fear*. Come with us and we'll share our *plans*. When you know them, you'll be *a fan*."

"Fan and plans don't really rhyme, now do they?" Nina said. "And no, I won't go anywhere with you. I told you I'd like to interview you, and I still want to do that. But here, at school."

"Not *unprepared*, she truly is *scared*," Bellamy said with a mean laugh.

"We're about to be *famous*, and you could have *claimed us*," Kaleb said. "We have a *room-ful* of *stuff*, but—" he stopped and turned to Bellamy.

"But she's not *tough enough*," she finished.

"What kind of stuff? What room? And why are you about to be famous?" Nina asked.

"Oh, no, no, no!" Kaleb scolded, shaking his finger like an old-fashioned teacher. His voice switched from the playful singsong he had been using to a harsh, aggressive tone. "You don't get just a little taste. You want to know what we're up to? Meet us on the hill after school on Thursday. You wait there, and we'll find you. We can talk for a while and see where it goes."

The hill was a slope behind Capital Central High School, where the students liked to meet and hang out. Nina felt comfortable with the plan since there were usually other students chilling out there.

"What do you mean, 'where it goes'?" she asked.

"You can decide if you want to see our stuff.

And we'll decide if you can be trusted with our secret," Kaleb said.

"All right," Nina said. "I'll meet you there on Thursday after school."

Bellamy and Kaleb left. She was alone in the hallway. She shivered a little. They were strange. And more than a little scary. They looked so different. They were obviously planning something. Nina wondered what it was.

She thought of all the school shootings that had made the news over the past few years. How the students responsible had been planning their killings for some time. Stockpiling weapons. How students at their schools always said the shooters seemed "different." Misfits. Bellamy and Kaleb matched the image. They didn't fit in with the rest of Cap Central's students. They were clearly planning something. And they mentioned that they had "stuff."

Maybe if she could get Bellamy and Kaleb to trust her, they would tell her what they were planning.

And maybe she could prevent it.

JAIR

I think it might be broken," Jair said, sitting in the kitchen with his right foot on a chair.

"Tell me again how it happened?" his mother asked.

"I tripped on the stairs coming up," he said. "It really hurts."

Lying to his mother felt bad. But to be convincing, he needed crutches and some sort of bandage or something from an actual doctor.

"I guess we'd better get you an x-ray," his mother said. "I wonder if Jarrold could come watch the boys."

Thinking about his uncle made Jair remember that he needed his right foot to practice driving. While his mother went to look for her cell phone, he put his right foot on the floor and his left foot on the chair.

"Okay, Jarrold's going to be here in a half hour," Jair's mother said. "Sit tight till then."

Jair reached for his phone. While he waited, he read the posts on the *Convo* blog. People were no longer talking about the thefts and other incidents at school. He wondered if Nina had gotten any more emails.

The door to the apartment opened and Jarrold walked in. Royce and Marcel, Jair's younger brothers, threw themselves at their uncle. Jair wished he could hang with Jarrold, but getting people's sympathy was more important to him.

As he wrestled with the little boys, Jarrold tried to have a conversation with Jair. "So, what'd you do?" he asked.

"It wasn't anything much," Jair said. "Just tripped on the steps."

"Did you fall all the way down?" Jarrold asked him.

"Nah. Just tripped. And twisted it. Might be broken, though," Jair said.

"We should go," Mrs. Nobles said.

"How about I give you a ride?" Jarrold asked.

"The kids are already dressed for bed," Mrs. Nobles said tiredly.

"They don't mind going out in pj's, do you, guys?" Jarrold said to the little boys. "And anyway, Batman and Spidey will protect us, right?"

Royce was wearing Batman pajamas, while Marcel's pajamas looked like a Spider-Man suit.

The whole family piled into Jarrold's car. Jair was squished in the back with his brothers. Jarrold pulled up in front of the 24-hour walk-in clinic on Florida Avenue. Jair and his mother got out.

The waiting room was busy. When it was finally Jair's turn, the examination itself went quickly. The doctor couldn't feel any swelling or breaks of any kind, so she didn't even take an x-ray. But she did direct Mrs. Nobles to buy Jair an ankle brace to keep it immobilized until he felt better. She also suggested crutches.

They stopped at a CVS on the way home and bought the two items. Jair felt really guilty. He had thought the doctor would just give them the crutches and brace, sort of like getting a free bandage after a shot. He never expected that his mother would have to pay for the items. But by that time, it was too late to tell the truth.

The next morning Jair took extra pains with his appearance. He knew people would be looking at him, so he wanted to look good.

He took the bus to school. An older lady was sitting in the handicapped seat. He stared at her, and she moved her bags over to make room for him. At the school's bus stop, he balanced on the crutches while he put on his backpack.

As he approached the school's entrance, he saw Joss and Eva.

"Hey, do you need help?" Joss asked, looking concerned. She held the door open for him.

"J, what happened?" Eva asked.

Jair grimaced, as if in pain.

"Craziest thing," he said. "This lady was trying to cross the street with a stroller and a little kid. Light turned red, cars started to go, and she couldn't get the stroller up on the curb. I saw what was happening and ran across the street to help. Got the stroller on the sidewalk just in time."

It was a complete and utter lie. His story did

not include even a shred of truth. But when he saw the sympathetic looks on Eva's and Joss's faces, he knew it was worth it.

"Oh my gosh!" Eva said. "You weren't hit by a car, were you?"

"No, but the light had turned green and cars were starting to come my way. The curb was higher than I thought, and I went down."

"Oh, J," Joss gasped. "You could have been killed!"

By this time, a small crowd had formed.

"Or the mother and her kids could have been hit," Neecy said. "Thank goodness you were there."

"Well, no worries," Jair said modestly. "Anybody else would have done the same thing."

"I don't think so," Joss said. "She's lucky you were there. Somebody else might have just walked away."

"So where did this happen?" Nina asked.

Jair hadn't even realized she had joined the group. She was standing to the side, where he hadn't seen her.

"Um, on H Street," he said, scrambling to come up with a street name.

"What time of day?" she asked.

"Well, officer, I think it was about five," Jair said sarcastically. "What is this anyway?"

"Just trying to picture it, that's all," Nina said. "I'm a journalist, remember?"

Jair didn't like her tone. He turned back to the rest of the group. "Well, the late bell's going to ring," he said. He made a big show of trying to balance his backpack while using the crutches.

"Here, man, I can take that," Carlos Garcia said, pulling the backpack off Jair's shoulders. "Want to stop at your locker before going to your first class?"

"Thanks, man," Jair said. "I 'preciate the help."

He hobbled into school surrounded by the group of students. These were the people he wanted to be friends with. But it seemed like they only liked him when he was rescuing somebody. Or injured. He saw Luther Ransome standing inside. Luther nodded but walked on.

Carlos helped him into Mr. Sullivan's math class. They took their seats. As soon as the pledge of allegiance was over, Mrs. Dominguez called into the room to ask Jair to come to the office.

"I can help," Melinda Stevens said.

She stood up and waited while Jair packed up his backpack. Then she walked with him to the office.

Jair tried hard to sound normal, but inside he was frightened. He had no idea why the office wanted him to come down.

When he got there, Mrs. Dominguez asked him to take a seat and wait for Mrs. Hess. Jair thanked Melinda and she left.

"While you're waiting, Jair, let me get you an elevator key," Mrs. Dominguez said. "How long are you going to be on crutches?"

"Not sure," Jair said, hopping over to take the key. "It's not broken, so it's pretty much up to me and how it feels."

"Well, use the key as long as you're on crutches," Mrs. Dominguez said. "Just don't forget to give it back to me."

"Thanks," Jair said.

He sat back down. Then Mrs. Hess's door opened. "Jair, we're ready for you," she said.

He hobbled into her office. Mrs. Hess and Mr. Gable were standing behind her desk, looking at the computer screen.

"Jair, we need you to tell us again what happened the day of the fire," Mrs. Hess said. "What you saw, where you were, everything."

"Sure," Jair said. He hoped he sounded more confident than he felt. "Not much to tell. My stomach felt bad, so I asked Doctor Miller if I could go to the restroom. I got there and found the fire. I ran back and told Doctor Miller."

"Didn't you tell me you saw Kaleb Black leaving the restroom?" Mr. Gable asked.

"Yeah, I thought I saw him in the hall," Jair said. "I might have the timing wrong, though. I see him up there a lot." Jair knew they had probably already looked at the video from the security camera. Kaleb hadn't been in the hall when Jair set the fire, so he had to get out of the lie.

"Well, it's hard for us to see who was in the restroom at the time," Mr. Gable said. "Watch this with us, and tell us if you know any of these people."

Jair watched the video. He saw a group of guys go into the restroom. It was a large bunch. Right in the middle was a figure with his head down, wearing a dark hoodie. Jair knew it was him. His face never showed on the camera. Soon the group of guys left, but the figure in the hoodie did not reappear.

Nothing happened for a while, and then a class of students entered the frame. As they walked past, the restroom door opened. Jair watched the dark figure walk out and mingle with the class. The camera did not catch where he went.

A short while later he saw himself walk into the hall heading toward the restroom, his face in full view. He saw himself look at the camera. He flinched. He wished he hadn't been so obvious. He saw himself open the door, close it again, and run down the hall. Mr. Gable turned off the tape.

"Any idea who the kid in the hoodie is?" he asked.

"What kid?" Jair asked.

"Roll it back," Mrs. Hess said.

Mr. Gable backed the tape up quickly. Then he rolled it again. He pointed to the figure in the hoodie. "Recognize him?"

"I can't really see him," Jair said, looking intently at the screen. "Do you think that's who set the fire?"

"Seems like it," Mr. Gable said. "Didn't really

seem like the right height to be Kaleb. Though we can't tell for sure how tall the guy is. This film's pretty bad."

"Can't help you," Jair said. "Sorry. He wasn't around when I got to the restroom."

"Shame you didn't see more," Mr. Gable said. "We want to catch this guy. This fire? Could have done some real damage if you hadn't found it."

Jair couldn't tell if Mr. Gable was giving him credit for saving the situation. It didn't really sound like it. It sounded more like an accusation.

"What happened to your foot?" Mr. Gable asked.

"Twisted my ankle," Jair said.

"How?"

Jair wasn't going to tell them the made-up story. "Tripped on a curb," he said.

"Are we done here?" Mrs. Hess asked Mr. Gable. "I have another meeting."

"Yeah, we're done. For now," Mr. Gable said. "But we're not done with this investigation," he said to Jair. "We got lots of other evidence. You think of anything else, you let me know, hear?

We're pretty close to catching this guy, and when we do, he's going away for a long time."

Jair went back to class. He wished he'd never set the fire. He was more scared than he'd ever been in his life.

CHAPTER 11

NINA

Wednesday lunch, Nina took her usual seat by Joss and Eva. Keisha Jackson sat down across from them. Nina turned to Joss. "Listen, I just wanted to let you know that tomorrow after school—"

Before she could finish, Keisha said, "Oh! Wait a second." She jumped up and walked toward the cafeteria doors.

Nina looked to see what had startled her. Jair was entering the cafeteria on his crutches, looking at the line helplessly.

As Nina watched, Keisha said something to Jair, who nodded and smiled. Then Keisha and Jair went to the front of the line. Keisha said something to the students behind them, who stepped back to let them pass.

"If I ask you guys something, will you answer me honestly? And keep it in confidence?" Nina asked Joss and Eva.

"Sure," Eva said. Joss nodded.

"Do you actually believe Jair's story? Do you think his ankle is really hurt?"

Joss's eyes got large. "Who would make up a story like that? And why?" she asked. "Yes, I totally believe him."

Eva looked perplexed. "I do too," she said. "He's a good guy. He wouldn't lie about something like that. Why? What do you know?"

Nina shook her head. "Nothing," she said. "It just seemed strange to me, that's all. First Keshawn, and then Jair."

"But for totally different reasons," Joss said. "Keshawn tripped over an old lady's cat, and Jair hurt his helping that woman with her kids." Her eyes narrowed. "Boy, are you ever suspicious."

"You're right," Nina said. "I guess I am suspicious these days. I think it's from working on the *Star*. And speaking of the paper, I need to tell you guys something. Keep it to yourselves, but I want someone to know. I'm interviewing Kaleb and Bellamy tomorrow after school."

"Oh my gosh," Eva said breathlessly. "Are you sure that's safe? Now *they're* the ones I'm suspicious of."

"That's why I'm talking to them here," Nina said. "I'm meeting them on the hill, so I'm sure there will be people around. I just wanted some-one to know."

"In case what? You *are* worried, aren't you?" Joss said. "How about if we hang out there, just to keep an eye on things?"

"Seriously?" Nina said. "I think I can handle it. But if they find my body in a dumpster, cut up into little pieces …"

Joss playfully punched her in the arm. "Just promise us you won't do anything stupid," she said. "Stay on the hill. And don't go anywhere with them."

"I'm not going anywhere," Nina said. "I just have to figure out what to ask them."

"Ask them what their story is," Eva said. "Why they talk in rhymes. What they write in their notebooks. Why they dress like that. And the most burning question of all, ask Bellamy where she buys her lipstick."

"And who does her hair," Joss added.

"Okay, good questions all." Nina laughed. She looked down toward the end of the table. Keisha set Jair's tray down and held his crutches while he took his seat. Then Durand Butler and Rainie Burkette came in, followed by Keshawn Connor. Durand set Keshawn's tray down, and they all sat.

"You guys look like you were in a war zone," Joss called out to them.

Jair shook his head sheepishly. "It is such a pain," he said. "Right?" he asked Keshawn.

"A pain in more ways than one," Keshawn said. "I seem to bump this thing about every five minutes."

"Yeah, right?' Jair said, agreeing with Keshawn. "Every five minutes."

Nina was quiet. She was still convinced there was nothing wrong with Jair's leg. She had seen him watching Keshawn and getting attention.

CHAPTER 12

JAIR

Jair wished lunch could go on forever. He loved being in the middle of this group of Cap Central kids. He knew their attention was based on a lie. But it didn't matter. He hadn't been able to join this crowd any other way. The fear he had felt in Mrs. Hess's office melted away as everyone fussed over him.

When the bell rang, he stood to clear his tray. He nearly bumped into Melinda Stevens.

"You going to class?" she asked.

He nodded.

"Let me help," she said, taking his tray.

Jair got his crutches in place and walked beside her.

"Did you do that homework for Ms. B?" he asked.

"No, I had an Explorers meeting last night," she said. "I'll do it tonight. It's not due till tomorrow."

"What're Explorers?" Jair asked.

"I'm in the Explorers Post. We learn police stuff, like accident investigation and how to use equipment. We also do lots of community service projects."

"Boy, you're really into this stuff, aren't you?" Jair said.

"I just really want to be a police officer," Melinda said. "Either that or serve in the military."

"Why?" Jair asked curiously.

"I like helping people," Melinda said. "Makes me feel good."

"So do the cops keep track of the stuff you do? Like when you help people?" Jair asked.

"What do you mean?" Melinda asked.

"Like, is there some sort of record of good stuff that you get credit for, that they'll look at when you apply to be a cop?"

Melinda looked confused. "Not really," she said. "Not that I know of. It doesn't really come up. It's not like we have a good deeds report or anything like that."

"Then how do you get them to know you've done good stuff?"

"They don't," Melinda said. "Nobody knows what I do or don't do. Except for me. And whoever I help."

"But don't you want people to know? Isn't that part of why people do good stuff? Heroes and all?" Jair asked.

"Not me," Melinda answered. "And probably not most people. Are you saying that if you saw someone who needed help, but no one would know you helped, you wouldn't bother?"

Jair didn't like how that sounded. "No, I'd help them," he said hesitantly. "I mean, yes, of course I would help. It's not about anyone else knowing," he lied.

"Look, I think you should do a ride-along," Melinda said. "Go out with the cops and see what they do. I'm scheduled to do one Saturday night. Why don't you sign up too? We can do the ride-along. When we're done, we can grab a pizza or something and talk about it."

Jair looked at her for a moment. "Did you just ask me out?" he asked.

"You're trippin'," she said.

Jair shook his head with a smile. "Nah. You asked me out," he said.

Melinda rolled her eyes. "You are living in a dream world," she said, shaking her head. "But anyway, suit yourself. If you want to go with me, let me know. I can pick you up. Since you can't walk and all. In fact, it's possible they might not want you to do it until your leg is better."

"It's actually getting better," Jair said quickly. "I can probably do it."

"Give me your hand," Melinda said, taking out a pen.

Jair stuck his hand out. Melinda wrote a phone number on his palm.

"That's my cell. If you want to do this, let me know. I'll get you the number where you need to call for permission to sign up."

The bell rang, signaling the start of class.

"Still sounds like a date to me," Jair said, walking into class.

"Dream on," Melinda answered.

CHAPTER 13

NINA

Nina was the last to arrive at the usual table in the cafeteria on Thursday. She sat down beside Joss. The table was unusually quiet. She noticed that all her friends were looking at her.

"Okay, what's going on?" she asked.

"We're just worried about you," Neecy Bethune said. "I can't believe you're going to be with the BKs after school by yourself."

"You told everyone?" Nina said to Joss.

"I just thought everyone should be looking out for you," Joss said.

"Give me a break," Nina scoffed. "What do you think, that they're going to murder me on the hill?"

"Who knows?" Eva said darkly. "I don't trust them."

Nina rolled her eyes. "You guys are unbelievable," she said.

"Promise us you won't go anywhere with them," Joss said. "And that you'll text me when you're home afterward."

"Where would I go?" Nina said. "We're sitting on the hill, talking. That's all."

"Promise," Joss said. "If I don't hear from you, I'm calling the cops."

"Seriously?" Nina said incredulously. "Okay, I promise. I'll text you when I'm done. Now, can I just eat my lunch?"

"I've got to go talk to Mrs. McArdle about the Poms meeting," Eva said, referring to the sponsor of the Poms team. She walked over to Nina and gave her a hug. "*Vaya con Dios.*"

"I'm not going into a battle zone," Nina said with a smirk. "Really. I think you'll see me again. Right here. Same time tomorrow."

"Yeah, but you might have hacked off your hair and be wearing bright red lipstick and a black cape," Eva said.

"So one conversation and I cross over to the dark side?" Nina laughed.

"You never know," Eva said as she left.

Nina finished her lunch. "Okay," she said, standing up. "So if I don't come back, tell my parents that I love them, and—"

"Oh, stop!" Joss said, giggling. "Just text me, okay?"

Nina left the cafeteria. As she walked out, she passed Jair. He no longer used his crutches, but he was still limping. After she passed him, she realized it had been a while since she had heard of anyone having their wallet or phone stolen. It was odd that it had just stopped. She wondered if the questions she had been asking had scared Jair—or whoever was responsible— into stopping.

She still wanted to write a story about the crimes. But right now she had to focus on her conversation with Bellamy and Kaleb. She went to the library and found a quiet table in the back. She sat and looked at her notes.

She knew what she wanted to learn. She wanted to know why they tried to look so unusual. She wanted to know if their sinister appearance was meant to scare people.

But mostly, she wanted to know if they were plotting something against the school and its students and teachers.

Because despite how confident she acted in front of her friends, Bellamy and Kaleb scared her. If they were planning to pull off something spectacularly horrifying, she wouldn't be surprised.

CHAPTER 14

JAIR

As Jair walked into the cafeteria, he passed Nina walking out. She hadn't spoken to him in a while about the incidents at the school. He hoped she had moved on to something else.

He hobbled over to where Luther Ransome, Chance Ruffin, and Thomas Porter sat at their regular table. As he approached, he heard Thomas say, "Left it right there, middle of Bladensburg Road. Flat empty at that point. Just got out and ran. Heard this loud crash and—"

Thomas quit talking as Jair sat down.

Jair looked around. The three guys were looking at him. "What?" he asked.

"You been talking to that girl. Melinda something?" Luther Ransome said.

"I know her, that's all," Jair said. He wasn't

sure why Luther was asking. He didn't want to admit they were becoming friends.

"You know she wants to be a cop, right?" Chance said.

"Yeah, heard that," Jair said. "She's in some of my classes." He gave a dismissive laugh. "Not like I like her or anything."

"We need to watch what we say around you?" Thomas asked.

Jair laughed hard. Even to him, it sounded fake. "Course not," he said. "Like I'd tell her anything!"

Thomas looked at him hard. Jair thought it was the coldest look anyone had ever given him. Then Thomas nodded once. He got up and left the table.

"You heard about the party Saturday?" Luther asked.

"Nah," Jair answered. "Where?"

"Janelle Minnerly's," Luther answered.

"Man, that girl never learns," Jair said, shaking his head. It had been at a party at Janelle's where he and Zander Peterson had rescued Keisha Jackson when she was surrounded by older guys trying to force her to drink. Another group of strangers had dragged Janelle into a bedroom. He and Zander had burst in just in time.

"So you going?" Luther asked.

"Yeah, sure," Jair said.

Luther nodded. He stood up. Chance stood up as well. They both walked away, leaving Jair sitting by himself.

He didn't know how he'd get out of his plans with Melinda. But when it came to a choice, he'd rather hang with these guys. She was just a cop wannabe.

CHAPTER 15

NINA

As soon as school was out, Nina headed for the hill. She sat down on an old lawn chair someone had left. Gradually, more students came out. Some tossed Frisbees. Others just sat in small groups and talked. She looked around, but she didn't see Bellamy or Kaleb.

She took out *The Grapes of Wrath* and tried to read. She was very tense and read the same paragraph over and over.

Fifteen minutes passed, and then a half hour. She was getting angry. Fewer students were left on the hill. She thought about leaving. If Bellamy and Kaleb weren't going to show up, she didn't want to waste any more time.

She pulled out her phone to check for messages. Nothing. She tucked her phone back in her pocket. Finally, after more than forty-five minutes, she decided to leave. She closed her book.

"Boo!" Bellamy and Kaleb yelled.

Nina jumped, nearly knocking her chair over. The two stood on either side of her. She hadn't heard them come up. Her heart was pounding.

"You guys scared me to death," she said, her voice sounding shaky.

Kaleb gave an crazed laugh. "Not quite," he said. "Seeing how you're still with us."

"I wouldn't have been in another minute," Nina said. Her shock had turned to anger. "I've been sitting here since school let out. I didn't think you were coming."

"Oh, we wouldn't have missed it," Bellamy said. "This is our big day."

"What do you mean?" Nina asked.

"You, of course," Kaleb said. "You're going to hear our message. Spread it to the world."

Nina felt a little shiver of fear. "So what's your message?"

Kaleb and Bellamy looked at each other.

"Not yet," Kaleb said. "Ask other questions

first." He sat down on the grass beside Nina's chair. Bellamy sat next to him.

Nina felt like she was sitting on a throne above them. "This is awkward," she said. "Do you want to sit on the steps?"

"We'd rather leave," Bellamy said. "To show you what you need to know about us. About our plans."

Nina was not going to go anywhere with these two. "I want to stay here," she said. She got out of the chair and sat beside them on the grass. She pulled out her notebook. "So, talk," she said. "Tell me why you wear those clothes."

"What do you mean?" Kaleb said. "What clothes?"

"Well, you know," Nina said. It was sort of an uncomfortable question. "Why do you wear the clothes you wear?"

"Why do you wear the clothes you wear?" Bellamy echoed.

"My clothes?" Nina asked. "I dress like everybody else."

"That's pretty pathetic," Kaleb said. "We choose not to."

"But you choose clothes that scare people," Nina said.

"If people are scared by our clothes, that's their problem, not ours," Bellamy said. "Next question."

"Some people wonder if maybe you're—" Nina stopped. She felt uncomfortable asking what might look like an accusation. "Some people think you might be behind all these thefts and other stuff."

Kaleb looked at Bellamy with a confused expression. "What thefts? What other stuff?" he asked. "What are you talking about?"

"The phones and wallets that keep disappearing. The false fire alarms. The fire last week in the school," Nina said.

Bellamy laughed bitterly. "Unbelievable," she said. "So because people don't like how we dress, they're blaming us for everything that goes on here? How very convenient."

"Actually, we did do all those things," Kaleb said. "And more. The earthquake last year? Us. The forest fires? Us again. Also the Kennedy assassination, and—"

"Stop," Nina said. "I get the point. But you've got to admit, you act mysterious. You're always writing in your notebooks. People think—"

"People think? People think? Who are these people, and why are you listening to them?" Bellamy asked. "You've started every question with 'people think.' What do *you* think?"

"I don't know," Nina said. "You just seem to have … to have something going on," she said, stammering a bit. "I'm just curious about what it is."

Kaleb and Bellamy looked at each other. Bellamy nodded slightly. Then Kaleb nodded as well. It was as if they had asked each other a question, and then answered it, all without speaking.

"Here's the thing," Kaleb said slowly. "We do have something going on."

"We have a plan," Bellamy said. "A big plan. We write in our notebooks as we make changes or add to it. It doesn't have anything to do with missing cell phones or false fire alarms. It's lots bigger than that."

"So, what is it?" Nina asked. She felt a

combination of excitement and apprehension. She wanted to know what they were up to. But she was worried about what they might tell her.

"It would be a lot better if we showed you," Kaleb said.

He stood up and brushed off the seat of his pants. He reached down and held his hand out to Bellamy. She stood up as well. Kaleb held out his hand to Nina.

"What are you doing?" Nina asked.

"We need to take you to … to where we work on our plan," Bellamy said. "It's not here. Are you coming?"

"No," Nina said sharply. "Let's just talk here. Tell me what the plan is."

"Better if we show you," Kaleb said. "Easier for you to see our supplies. What we plan to do with it all. If we just told you… Well, it wouldn't be the same," he said, shrugging. "Not as spectacular as seeing it all for yourself."

Nina didn't know what to do. She wanted to know what they were planning, and she was the one who had asked for them to tell her. But she was still scared. She didn't want to go anywhere with them. She tried to stall. "Do we have to do it now?" she asked. "Do you have some sort of deadline?"

"Actually, we do," Bellamy said. "December twenty-eighth. That's our D-Day."

"So where is all your stuff?"

"Not far," Kaleb said. "Coming? You won't be sorry. When you see what we're cooking up, you'll realize how lucky you are that you're the one we trusted. That we made you part of it."

Nina didn't know what to say. If they were planning some sort of crime against Cap Central, she wanted to know so she could prevent it. But she still didn't want to leave the school with either of them.

"I promise," she said. "But please, can't we just stay here and talk? I'm not really supposed to leave school except to go home."

"Your choice," Bellamy said. "Come with us and learn our plans. Stay here and never know. What's it going to be?"

Nina knew she shouldn't go with them. Everything about them screamed danger. The safe choice was to stay here at school.

"Let's go," she said, standing up.

CHAPTER 16

JAIR

Jair left school and headed toward the bus stop. His crutches were really starting to annoy him. He was sorry he had ever pretended to have hurt his foot.

At the bus stop an older lady was sitting on the bench. She was surrounded by grocery bags. She saw him and got slowly to her feet.

"Here, sugar, you sit," she said.

He looked around. No one he knew was at the stop. "Okay," he said, taking her seat.

She stood, leaning against the side of the bus shelter for support.

Jair immediately felt terrible. There was nothing wrong with him, and the lady looked like a strong wind could blow her over.

He stood up again. "Actually, you should sit," he said. "My leg feels better when I'm standing."

"Well, bless you," the woman said, sitting back down. "I am feeling pretty tired this afternoon."

The bus arrived and Jair waited for the older woman to get on. She sat on the handicapped seat and moved over so there was room for him.

"I'm good," he said, hobbling down to another open seat.

He stared out the window. He didn't know what to do about Saturday night. On the one hand, Luther Ransome and Chance Ruffin had been his friends for a long time. Or as close to friends as those guys got. He knew they weren't the kind of people he could ever count on. In fact, they had turned against him once before, back when Zander Peterson had first come to Cap Central and Jair had tried to fight him.

As for Thomas Porter, Jair knew he was trouble. Jair didn't really care about Thomas. But Luther and Chance? They were star athletes. Girls liked them. And without being an athlete himself, Jair knew he didn't have any chance of sharing their glory.

But he was starting to like Melinda. She was … He tried to figure out why he enjoyed talking to her. Certainly she wasn't the most beautiful girl in school. She didn't really stand out one way or another. The main thing he liked about her was that she was interesting. She was committed to something. She knew who she was and what she wanted. Jair didn't know anyone else like her.

When he arrived home, he found his uncle stretched out on the couch, asleep.

"Shhh," his mother whispered after he shut the door. "Let him sleep. He worked a bad one last night."

"What happened?" Jair asked.

"Some terrible accident," his mother said. "Lots of injuries. He's staying for dinner, but let him sleep for now."

Jair went into his bedroom. He took the soft boot off his foot and put his shoe on. He stuck the boot in his closet, along with the crutches. He could hear his mother in the kitchen. He checked the time on his phone. He knew it was about time for his younger brothers to be getting off the school bus at the end of the block.

He walked into the kitchen. "I'll go meet the bus," he said.

His mother looked at him in surprise. "I was about to go," she said. "What about your ankle?"

"It's better," he answered. "I got this."

He walked down the street and waited till the yellow school bus pulled up. His brothers piled out, along with other young children.

"Where's Mom?" Marcel asked.

"At home," Jair answered.

"Why isn't she here?" Royce asked.

" 'Cause I am," Jair said. "Let's go."

The younger boys walked ahead of him toward the apartment. Despite Jair's mother's attempts to keep them quiet, they made enough noise to wake up their uncle.

Jarrold played with the younger boys for a bit, then turned to Jair.

"You need to practice driving in rush hour," he said. "Want to go out now?"

"Sure," Jair said. "Let me get my permit."

"Wait. What about the ankle?" Jarrold asked.

"It's almost all better," Jair answered. "And anyway, it was my left ankle."

"But if you're not one-hundred percent," Jarrold said.

"Nah, I am," Jair said. I took off the brace. No worries."

"Let's go, then," Jarrold said. "You need to finish your hours."

"Be back for dinner," Jair's mother said.

"Don't worry," Jarrold said.

They got in the car. Jair drove down Sixteenth Street. "Where to?" he asked.

"I don't care. Just drive," Jarrold said. "I'm just going to relax. I'm fried," he added.

"Mom said you worked a bad one last night," Jair said, turning left onto Mt. Olivet Road.

"Yeah. It was tough," Jarrold said. "Whole family coming home from celebrating a kid's birthday at Taco Bell. Some idiot ran out of gas on Bladensburg Road and just left the car. No flashers, nothing."

Jair slammed on the brakes. "Bladensburg Road?" he said. "Last night?"

"Hey, easy," Jarrold said. "Don't be going so fast that you need to stop like that. Ease into it.

But yeah, right near New York Avenue. Guy just jumped out, right before this family came along. They plowed into the back of it, and the birthday kid was hurt real bad."

Jair felt sick. He remembered Thomas Porter talking at lunch about abandoning a car along Bladensburg Road and hearing a crash.

"Kid going to make it?" Jair asked.

"Gonna take a while, but yeah," his uncle said. "Wish we knew who the guy was who jumped out. Lots of stolen cars lately. Usually abandoned on some side road. This was a new one. With all the cameras around? We'll get the guy. Somebody knows something, and we'll hear it eventually. With any luck, the guy left prints inside."

Jair considered telling his uncle what he knew. But even though it was his uncle, he didn't want to be a snitch. "Hope they get him," he said. "Hey, I'm thinking of doing a ride-along this Saturday night," he said, changing the subject. "What do I have to do?"

"I'll set it up," Jarrold said. "I can call you tomorrow with the details."

They drove together for a while, talking

about sports and other things. Traffic was bad, and they finally turned around.

Right near the high school, Jair waited at a red light at the complicated Starburst inter-section, where Florida Avenue intersected with Benning and Bladensburg roads, and with H Street. As the light turned green, he waited for pedestrians to cross. With a start, he realized Bellamy and Kaleb were among those crossing. And Nina Ambrose was with them.

"Son, when the light is green, it means to go," Jarrold said as someone behind Jair honked angrily.

Jair drove slowly through the intersection. He wondered what was going on.

CHAPTER 17

NINA

Where are we going?" Nina asked.

"This way," Kaleb said, heading down the hill.

Nina pulled out her phone. "I need to know where we're going," she said again. She wanted to text the address to Joss.

"It's not far," Bellamy said. "Come on."

Nina stopped. "Not until you tell me where we're going," she said.

"H Street," Bellamy said. "Now let's go."

Nina sent a quick text to Joss. Within seconds, she heard a chime, signaling a response. She knew without even reading it that Joss was telling her not to go. She silenced her phone and put it back in her pocket.

When they got to H Street, Bellamy and

Kaleb turned left. They walked about a block. Nina saw the bright blue awning that hung over Nanny's Place, a popular restaurant. Nina hoped they were going to walk into the restaurant.

Instead, Kaleb and Bellamy turned into an alley that ran alongside the building. The alley was dark, with dumpsters lining both sides.

Nina paused. "Where does this go?" she asked with more than a little fear.

"You'll see," Kaleb said. "Come on." He walked about halfway down the alley until he got to a door. He pulled out his phone and sent a text. Then he took out a key and unlocked the door. "This way," he said.

Nina knew she shouldn't go in. Everything about this was wrong. She was interviewing Bellamy and Kaleb because they seemed sinister. Now she was about to go with them through a door in an alley. She wished she'd never decided to talk to them. She wanted to turn and run. But she felt trapped.

She didn't want to be rude or insulting. And she was still curious as to what they were about to show her. If going with them offered a chance to prevent a tragedy like a mass shooting, she didn't want to pass it up.

She stepped through the door. Inside was a steep flight of stairs. Kaleb and Bellamy started up the stairs. Nina followed. She could hear the sounds of a restaurant kitchen through the wall beside the stairs. The noises were reassuring. If she felt like she were in any danger, she could scream and someone in the kitchen would hear her. She hoped.

At the top of the stairs, Kaleb unlocked another door and went through. Bellamy followed him, while Nina hung back. Kaleb stuck his head out the door. "Are you coming?" he asked.

Nina reluctantly walked through the door. She stopped suddenly in surprise.

Inside was a beautiful apartment. It was filled with comfortable-looking furniture and brightly colored rugs on polished wood floors.

Nina looked around. This was nothing like what she had expected. It didn't match Kaleb's dark, ominous appearance.

She heard footsteps on the stairs behind

her. She turned. A small woman in a bright blue dress walked in. She was holding a tray.

"Hi, guys!" she said, setting the tray down on a counter in the kitchen. "Bells, how are you?" she said to Bellamy. "Hi," she said to Nina, sticking out her hand. "I'm Kaleb's mom, Nan Black."

"I … I'm Nina," Nina stammered. This was nothing like she had expected.

"Do you go to Cap Central too?" Nan Black asked.

"Mom, come on," Kaleb said. "We're hungry!"

"Well, dig in," his mother said with a laugh. "I didn't know what you wanted, so I brought a little of everything. There are sliders, chicken wings, and shrimp. Oh, I brought up some of those crab cakes you like, Bellamy."

Nina couldn't believe it. The tray was filled with small plates of food. It took her a minute to realize that Kaleb's mother must be the "Nanny" of Nanny's Place.

"Okay, thanks, now leave us alone, please," Kaleb said. He put his arm around his mother's shoulders and urged her to the door. "Don't you have work to do?" he asked jokingly.

"Well, we are a little busy downstairs," his

mother agreed. "But I get the hint. Let me know if you need anything else. Want Cokes? Juice?"

"Mom!" Kaleb yelled.

"All right, I'm going," Kaleb's mom said. "Nina, nice meeting you."

She shut the door, and Kaleb let out a sigh. "She drives me crazy," he said, shaking his head.

"Seriously?" Nina said. "That kind of crazy sounds pretty good to me. You eat like this all the time?"

Kaleb picked up a slider and took a bite. "Pretty much," he said. "She can cook, I'll give her that. But she never stops talking." He pushed a plate of crab cakes toward Nina. "Here," he said. "Let's eat, and then we'll show you what you came here to see."

Nina dipped a crab cake in cocktail sauce and ate it in one bite. Then she ate a slider and two chicken wings. Everything was delicious. She couldn't imagine being able to eat after-school snacks like this every day.

She had just started to relax when Kaleb put the dishes in the sink. "You have to wash your hands," he said to Nina.

This was unexpected. Nina walked to the sink and scrubbed her hands.

He handed her a towel. "Dry them completely," he ordered.

Nina dried her hands and handed the towel to him. Bellamy and Kaleb both washed and dried their hands too.

When they were all ready, Kaleb and Bellamy turned and looked at each other. "Ready?" Kaleb asked.

"I guess," Bellamy said. "Though it feels sort of weird to show anyone."

"We agreed," Kaleb said.

"We did," Bellamy said. "Let's do it."

She turned and headed down a hallway. Kaleb started to follow, then turned to Nina. "You ready to see our plans?" he asked.

Nina was scared. She had no idea what they were about to show her. But she couldn't back out now. "I guess so," she said, acting braver than she felt.

Kaleb took out a key. He unlocked a door and held it open. Bellamy walked in the room, then walked out again. "Wait," she said. "We need to blindfold her."

Nina started to back down the hallway. "No," she said sharply. "I get to see or I leave."

"Just till we lead you into the room," Bellamy said. "Then we take it off so you can see it all."

"It will be better that way," Kaleb agreed. "Just go along with us, okay?"

Nina almost felt like she was watching a character in a movie, as she made dangerous choice after dangerous choice. "Whatever," she said finally. She felt as if it was too late to back out of anything they suggested now.

Kaleb went into another room and came back with a brightly colored scarf. "Turn around," he ordered.

Nina turned around and felt him tie the scarf around her head. Then he took her left hand, and Bellamy took her right. They led her into the room.

"Pull off the blindfold," Bellamy ordered.

Nina pulled off the scarf and looked around. She was speechless. Hanging all over the room were large pieces of white paper. The papers were covered with drawings. It was clearly a graphic novel. The drawings were precise, and colorful, and amazing.

Nina stepped closer and looked at the pictures. She recognized people in the drawings. There was a short guy in a baseball hat who looked a lot like Jair. There was a man who looked like a villain. He bore a resemblance to Mr. Gable, the school security officer. In one frame, someone was scribbling in a notebook. The character looked just like Nina.

"Is that me?" she asked.

"Yep," Bellamy said.

"This is amazing!" Nina said breathlessly. "What is it exactly?"

"It's our book," Kaleb said. "Books, actually. There are three here. The first three volumes of a series."

Nina couldn't take her eyes off the drawings. She recognized so many people from Cap Central. Luther Ransome, looking evil. Neecy Bethune whispering to Charlie Ray. Rainie Burkette, running. The drawings were so clear and realistic.

"Which one of you does the drawings?" she asked.

"That's all Bellamy," said Kaleb. "I do some of the writing, but we really both share that job."

Nina had never seen anything like it. "But I'm confused," she said finally. "I thought you said something about having a plan and a deadline."

"We do," Bellamy said. "There's a contest. The deadline is December twenty-eighth. Stan Lee's birthday."

"Who's Stan Lee?" Nina asked.

"You're kidding, right?" Kaleb said.

Nina shook her head.

"Only the most famous graphic artist in the world. You've maybe heard of Spider-Man? The Hulk? X-Men?" Kaleb said.

"Yeah, those guys I've heard of," Nina said. Now that she knew what the project was, and that it wasn't anything dangerous, she felt almost giddy with relief.

"Those are his creations. This contest is in his honor, since he is the best," Kaleb said.

"So what is the contest?" Nina asked.

"You have to submit a full-length graphic novel that could be turned into a series. It has to be completely finished. Writing, inking, everything," Bellamy said. "But we need your help with it."

"My help?" Nina asked. "How?"

"Here's the thing," Kaleb said. "People can vote online for the one they like best. The votes help determine the winner. We need people to support us, and we hoped you could write about us so that Cap Central students would vote for us."

"Oh my gosh!" Nina said. "People will be so relieved, of course they'll vote for you. Over and over again."

"Relieved?" Bellamy said. "Why relieved?"

"That you're not dangerous," Nina said. "That you're just artists."

"What did you think we were planning?" Kaleb asked curiously.

"I don't know," Nina said. "To blow up the school. Guns, bombs, whatever."

"Guns, bombs, *whatever*?" Bellamy said incredulously. "That's all, huh?" She shook her head in disgust.

"Look, this is great, and I'm happy to help," Nina said. "But you can't blame people for being a little suspicious. You guys talk in rhymes, sometimes you—"

"We're just always trying out characters and dialogue," Kaleb interrupted. "Look!" He walked over to a drawing. "Here's Hocus Pocus, one of the evil shape-changers who is out to get Strider, one of our heroes. Hocus uses rhyme to torture his enemies."

"What about the fire? What about—" Nina stopped. Now that she knew what they were working on, the rest of it sounded so stupid.

"What about what?" Bellamy asked.

"The wallets. The cell phones," Nina finished.

"We truly have no idea what you're talking about," Kaleb said. "We have one thing on our minds all the time. All day, all night. And that's this book. Even school just gets in the way. Bellamy is the most talented artist in the world, and—"

He stopped as Bellamy bowed dramatically.

"And Kaleb has an awesome imagination," Bellamy said. "But truly? That's all we think about. Oh, and his mother's crab cakes. I do think about them a lot."

Nina laughed. "I can see why," she said. "But your names. Why do you call yourselves the Black Knights?"

"We just came up with that as our ... our superhero artist identities," Kaleb said. "So when we write, we're not Kaleb and Bellamy. We step into the story in our minds. We become the Black Knights," he added in a deep, dramatic voice. "Does that make sense?"

"Maybe," Nina said. She wasn't sure she completely understood.

"Those are also our last names," Bellamy said. "So we were lucky. The Black Knights is a little cooler than calling ourselves 'the Smith Jones' or something like that, if we'd had lame last names."

"I wonder if you would have chosen other hobbies if you had different last names," Nina said. "So let's get down to business. I can write about this for the *Star*, right? And you'll give me a frame or two to run with the story. Oh, what do you get if you win?"

"Scholarships," Bellamy said. "Twenty thousand dollars each. To any college or art school we want to attend."

Nina whistled. "Then we've got to make sure you win," she said. "Now, tell me the story. Start to finish. And pick which frames you want to run in the paper."

She sat on Kaleb's bed and pulled out a

notebook. As a reporter, she could help Kaleb and Bellamy get the support they needed to help them in the contest. And could help others understand that they weren't at all dangerous. They were just different. She couldn't wait to get started.

CHAPTER 18

JAIR

Jair got to school a little early on Friday. As he walked down the half-empty hallway, someone called out his name. He turned and waited for Melinda Stevens to catch up to him.

"Heard you're doing a ride-along Saturday night," she said.

"How'd you hear that?" Jair asked.

"I heard your uncle called the station last night," she said. "He's a nice guy. I've seen him there before, but I never knew who he was."

"Yeah, he's great," Jair said.

"Want me to pick you up?" she asked.

"Sure," Jair said. "Hey, you ever see anybody you know get busted when you're on one of these ride-alongs?"

"Not yet," Melinda said. "But I've always

wondered if it's going to happen. That'd be pretty awkward."

"Wonder what they'd do?" Jair said. Knowing about the party at Janelle's Saturday night, he was worried the police car he rode in might respond if something went wrong.

"Well, it's not like they'd put criminals in the backseat with me sitting there," Melinda said. "They'd call for a transport. They'll do chases, though, with lights and sirens."

Jair thought it sounded like fun. "So what time should we go?" he asked.

"The shift is four hours, starting at six. I'll get you at fifteen till," Melinda said. "Text me your address." She started to walk down the hall.

"Next date, I'll pick *you* up," Jair said.

"Not a date, dude," Melinda said firmly.

"I think it is!" Jair called out after her.

Melinda just waved her hand without looking back.

Jair was still smiling as he turned around. He nearly bumped into Nina Ambrose, who was right behind him.

"So, you and Melinda," she said.

"Nah, we're friends is all," Jair said.

"Looked like a little more than friends to me," Nina teased.

"Yeah, well, you looked pretty friendly with the BKs last night too," Jair said.

He was glad to see how shocked Nina looked.

"How did you know about that?" Nina asked.

"Saw you walking down H Street," Jair said. "Sure wondered what you were up to."

"You could make a million guesses, and they'd all be wrong," Nina said hotly.

Jair decided to let it pass. He didn't care about fighting with Nina. "So how's that article coming?" he asked.

"How do you know about the article?" Nina asked. "I haven't even started writing it."

"You had asked me about it," Jair said, confused. "After the fire. About the phones."

"Oh, *that* article!" Nina said. "I've put it on hold. I'm working on something else."

"Did you ever figure out what was going on?" Jair asked.

"Nah," Nina said. "I think it has stopped. Curious, huh?"

"Maybe whoever was doing it just needed to borrow a phone," Jair said.

"And then leaving them around the school," Nina said. "Someday, I'd like to know why the person did it."

"Well, whatever the reason he was doing it, he's not doing it anymore," Jair said.

"So I guess you haven't been able to look like a hero as much since he stopped," Nina added.

"Wasn't looking for publicity," Jair said.

Funny. Since he'd started talking to Melinda and thinking about the police department, he hadn't even thought about stealing anything. He hoped Nina would drop the subject. It seemed like a lifetime ago.

CHAPTER 19

NINA

Nina knew Jair was lying. He had taken the things and then turned them in. But she knew she'd never be able to prove it. And now the thefts had stopped.

She walked down the hall toward first period. As she passed a short hallway that lead to the janitor's closet, she saw Kaleb and Bellamy, huddled together. Kaleb was holding a notebook.

"Hey!" she called out. "Working on the book?"

"Nah, this time we're planning some sort of incident," Kaleb joked. "You gave us the idea yesterday. Since everyone already thinks we're up to something and all."

"Yeah? What did you have in mind?" Nina asked, sitting beside them.

"We haven't gotten that far," Bellamy said.

"Maybe taking Mrs. Hess hostage until she agrees to give us Fridays off."

"Good luck with that," Nina said. She got up and brushed off her pants. "Hey, thanks for yesterday, by the way. It was fun. And the food was amazing. I'm still full."

"Whatever," Kaleb said. "Just make sure you spell our names right in your article."

"No problem," Nina said. "And I'll probably have lots of questions once I start writing."

Nina waved and went to class. She nearly laughed out loud. A day ago, she would have been frightened at the sight of Kaleb and Bellamy huddled over a notebook. Now that she knew what they were working on, she saw them in a whole new way.

She was so excited about writing their story. She had information that no one else at the school knew. When people read her article, they would realize how much they had misjudged the pair. Best of all, by writing about them, Nina could help them achieve their dream.

CHAPTER 20

JAIR

Jair slept late Saturday morning. When he woke up, he felt a little excited, as if something good were about to happen. He watched some cartoons with his brothers. When the cartoons were over, he asked them if they wanted to play soccer.

He took them to the Trinidad Recreation Center and kicked the ball to them for a while. He actually enjoyed playing with them. When the little boys realized he wasn't going to be mean to them, they began to relax. By the end of the afternoon, they were all having a good time.

They went back to their apartment, where Jair found his mother in the kitchen. He poured himself a glass of water. Then drank it. He rinsed out his glass. He saw that the dish drain was full of clean dishes. He began putting them away.

"Okay, what's up with you?" his mother asked, standing with her hands on her hips. "You feeling okay?"

"Seemed like you could use some help, that's all," Jair said, a little embarrassed.

"I can *always* use help, but I don't usually get any," his mother said, laughing. "And I've never known you to do anything with your brothers besides be mean to them," she added. "Whatever's causing these changes, I hope it lasts."

"Don't get too used to it," Jair said. "I'm sure Marcel and Royce will go back to being annoying before too long."

"Jarrold told me you're doing the ride-along tonight," his mother said. "He picking you up?"

"Nah, a friend's coming by," Jair said. "I'm leaving soon, actually. Around six or so. Oh, and I might be late. I think we're grabbing a pizza or something after."

"Sounds like fun," his mother said. "What's his name again?"

"Who?" Jair asked.

"The boy picking you up," his mother said.

"Oh. Not a boy," Jair said. He looked down at his shoes. "A girl. Melinda Stevens."

"Ah," his mother said, smiling.

"Don't look like that," Jair said. "Nothing to smile about. She's a friend, that's all."

"Um-hum," his mother said. "So what's she like?"

"She wants to be a cop," Jair said. "Uncle Jarrold knows her. You want to know all about her, ask your brother."

"I'm just kidding you," his mother said, kissing his cheek. "I'm sure she's a nice girl. And it sounds like a fun night. Probably the only thing you could choose to do where I'm not staring out my window, wondering where you are and whether you're safe."

"True that," Jair said with a grin. "I'm hitting the shower."

After his shower, he stared into his closet, wondering what to wear. He didn't want to look like he thought the evening was a date, but he also wanted to look good. Melinda was only a friend—so far. He liked talking to her. In fact, he felt more comfortable talking to her than he had ever felt talking to any other girl.

Melinda wasn't really part of any group at Cap Central. She was more of a loner. But everyone seemed to like her, and he could see why.

He pulled out a plaid shirt and his favorite jeans. He looked in the mirror. Usually he got angry when he saw his reflection. He was so short. But Melinda was petite. For the first time, it didn't matter that he wasn't tall.

His phone buzzed. A text. It was from Melinda, telling him she was in front of his apartment.

He grabbed his jacket and kissed his mother goodbye. He walked down the stairs and saw Melinda sitting in her car. He got in.

"So tell me how this works," he said.

Melinda told him what to expect. She drove along Bladensburg Road until she reached the Fifth District Station. She parked and they walked in together.

Melinda gave him a little wave as she walked off with the officers she would be riding with. Jair was assigned to Unit 5051 with Officers Bryant and Rodriguez. They went out to the parking lot and got in the car.

For the first part of the evening, they just rode around the streets in Northeast D.C. Jair enjoyed talking to the officers and listening to their joking back and forth.

All of a sudden, the radio crackled. "All available units, we've got a noise complaint at Eighteenth and K Northeast. Possible alcohol violations by juveniles. All units in the vicinity, please respond."

Officer Bryant replied, "10-4."

Officer Rodriguez turned around in his seat. "This'll be fun," he said with a grin.

"That's right near my school," Jair said.

Officer Bryant turned on his lights and siren. He began driving fast. He slowed down at intersections, but he went through them even if the light was red.

"So people are making noise?" Jair asked.

"It's a general disturbance call," Officer Rodriguez answered. "Sounds like a party."

Party.

All of a sudden, Jair knew why the address sounded familiar. It was Janelle's house. He would know people at the party.

"Uh, any way you could let me out before we get there?" he asked.

"Let you out?" Officer Bryant repeated. "Thought you wanted to see what being a police officer is all about. Why do you want to leave just when it gets fun?"

Jair didn't say anything. He sunk back into the seat of the car.

"Think you might know somebody?" Officer Rodriguez guessed.

"It's possible," Jair said.

"You can just stay in the unit if you like," Officer Bryant said. "You see anybody you know? Just look guilty, like we've arrested you. How's that? Because we can't let you out, for legal reasons. We have to get you back to the station, but right now we have to answer this call. Okay?"

Jair nodded. He stared out the window. Officer Bryant turned on K Street. Up ahead, Jair could see the flashing lights of other police cars. All of a sudden, a car came racing down the street toward them.

"All units, be advised, report of a vehicle stolen from the vicinity of Eighteenth and K streets Northeast," the dispatcher said. "Vehicle is an older model gray Honda Civic. D.C. plates." She listed the license plate number.

Up ahead, some police cars made U-turns and began chasing the car. "Are you kidding me?" Officer Rodriguez snorted. "All these units around? He thinks he's getting away?"

"We gonna chase it?" Jair asked.

"No, we're gonna work the party," Officer Bryant said. He parked his car at an angle. He picked up his radio. "Dispatch, this is Unit 5051. We're on the scene at 1032 Eighteenth Street. Be advised that we've got a civilian on board."

"Ten-4, 5051," the dispatcher said. "Unit 5051, officers need assistance administering field tests."

"Okay, we've got to make drunk kids breathe into a tube," Officer Bryant said. "You want to come watch?"

"Wish it was some other part of town," Jair said. "I think I'll just sit here and pretend to be a criminal."

"Suit yourself," Officer Rodriguez said, unbuckling his seat beat.

Jair was worried he'd be seen by someone

he knew. He sat low in the backseat, watching the activity. Jair thought about leaving. He reached for the door handle. Confused, he looked closer. There was no door handle. He realized that whoever was usually sitting in the backseat of the car was probably under arrest. They wouldn't want him to be able to escape.

"All units, be advised. Single vehicle accident on Florida Avenue at West Virginia Avenue Northeast. Possible injuries. EMTs en route."

Jair wondered what Melinda was doing. He pulled out his phone and sent her a text. She texted back that her car was heading for the accident site.

Some civilian cars began to arrive. They parked along the street. Adults got out and walked toward the party. After a while, he saw some of the same people walk back to their cars with a teen. He realized they were parents picking up their kids from the party.

One girl was crying as she walked past the police car. As another kid passed the car, he leaned over and vomited. Jair could hear pieces of the families' conversations as they passed.

Some kids were belligerent, while others

were apologetic. None of the parents looked happy. Some of the kids looked familiar, but Jair didn't really know any of them. He was glad Luther, Chance, and Thomas weren't among them. He wondered if they had attended.

Before too long, Officer Rodriguez returned. "Okay, we've got to get you back to the station house," he said. "But let's drive past that MVA to see what's going on."

"MVA?" Jair asked.

"Motor vehicle accident."

Officer Bryant got in and turned the car around. He drove down Florida to West Virginia Avenue. Traffic was backed up because of the accident. Officer Bryant turned on his lights and siren. Cars began moving out of his way. Jair loved it.

As they got close, Officer Bryant pulled the police car in at an angle and turned off the engine. He kept his lights flashing. "You coming?" he asked Jair.

"Can I?" Jair asked.

"Sure! Unless you think you know people here too?"

"Hope not," Jair said.

Officer Rodriguez opened the door and Jair got out. The scene was pretty bad. Three ambulances, fire trucks, lots of police cars. Jair could see the car flipped over on its side. A telephone pole was leaning over it at a dangerous angle. The car was a grey Honda. Jair figured it was the one in the earlier police dispatch. As he watched, he could see someone on a stretcher being placed in an ambulance.

Officer Bryant walked ahead. Jair hung back with Officer Rodriguez. Soon Officer Bryant returned. "You probably shouldn't get any closer," he said. "It's pretty bad."

"What happened?" Jair asked.

"Car versus pole. Pole's gonna win every time," Officer Bryant said. "Driver's drunk out of his mind. They were at that party, helped themselves to a car, and now this. And not a scratch on him. His friends weren't so lucky. They're pretty badly hurt."

"Do you know who they are?" Jair asked.

"Nah, didn't hear their names," Officer Bryant said. "Hope they're not folks you know."

Jair had a bad feeling. He hadn't seen Thomas Porter, Luther Ransome, or Chance

Ruffin come out of the party. He knew Thomas had started stealing cars. He hoped it wasn't them in the Civic.

They got back in the squad car and headed for the police station. Officer Bryant opened the back door of the car to let Jair out. "Did you enjoy your night?" he asked.

"It was great," Jair said. "Thanks!"

"You thinking about joining the academy?" Officer Rodriguez asked.

"Maybe," Jair said. "Seems like something I'd like to do."

"It's a great job," Officer Bryant said. "Any time you'd like to go out with us, let us know. You're welcome to come. Your uncle says you're good people. That's good enough for me!"

Jair saw Melinda walking out of the station house. He said goodbye to the officers and walked with her to her car.

"So?" she said as she drove out of the lot.

"That was awesome," Jair said.

"Yeah?" she said. "I thought you'd like it."

"Is it always like that?" he asked.

"Nah," she said. "Some nights nothing happens. This was a particularly good one."

"Did you get close enough to see who was in the car?" Jair asked.

"No, they wouldn't let me," Melinda said. "Hope it wasn't anyone we know."

She pulled up in front of Primo's and parked. They went in and ordered a pizza. As they ate, they talked and talked. Jair had never talked to any girl for that long before. He really liked her. He felt very comfortable.

All of a sudden, a man at the next table jumped to his feet. He put both hands on his throat. His face was contorted in fear. It was clear he was choking. The man's wife began screaming.

Jair jumped up. He grabbed the man from behind and squeezed hard. A piece of food flew from the man's mouth. He began gasping for air. He sank down into his chair, breathing heavily.

"Oh my gosh! Thank you!" the woman said. "Thank goodness you were here!"

"Thanks, son," the man said. "Think you saved my life!"

Jair felt shaky. He sat back down.

From across the room, he heard applause.

He looked in that direction. Charlie Ray and Neecy Bethune sat at a table.

"Way to go, J!" Charlie called out.

Jair waved. He was still too shaken to speak.

"Wow!" Melinda said with admiration. "Haven't you had a night."

Jair shook his head in amazement. "Never thought I'd actually get to do that," he said. "Thank you, Ms. Billingsley."

The older couple stopped by their table. "Thanks again," the man said. "I owe you!"

"No worries," Jair said. "Anybody'd have done the same."

"But not everyone knows how," the woman said. "Lucky for us, you were in the right place at the right time."

Jair and Melinda finished their pizza. Jair asked the waitress for the check.

"Honey, you're all settled up," she said. "Those older people paid it for you!"

Jair and Melinda looked at each other in surprise.

"And this night just gets better and better," Jair said.

Melinda drove to his apartment. She pulled up out front.

"Thanks," Jair said.

"For?" she asked.

"This. Everything," he said.

Melinda leaned over and kissed his cheek. Then she smiled.

Jair felt himself get all warm inside. He smiled back. "See ya," he said.

He got out of the car. He knew he was still grinning. But that was okay. This was about the best night of his life.

CHAPTER 21

NINA

It seemed like the whole school was talking about the accident and the party on Monday. Thomas Porter, who had been driving the Honda, had been arrested for stealing it and for driving drunk. Chance Ruffin and Luther Ransome had been injured.

Zakia Johnson, who had been in the front seat with Thomas, was pretty badly hurt. She was still in the hospital.

As far as Nina knew, none of her friends had been at the party. It was rumored that at least twenty kids had been cited for underage drinking. Even Janelle Minnerly's mother had been cited for allowing minors to drink alcohol in her house.

In journalism class, Nina asked her editors

for permission to write a news story about the party and the accident. She set aside the story about the BKs for a while to concentrate on the more immediate news.

She wanted to speak with someone who had actually been at the party. She thought over all the people she knew who might have been likely to attend. One name came to mind.

Jair.

He was friends with Thomas, Luther, and Chance. And he had gone to that other party at Janelle's house.

At lunch, she watched for him in the cafeteria. She saw him come in. She waited for him at the end of the food line.

"Can I talk to you a minute?" she asked.

"What's up?" he said curiously.

"Just wondered if you were at the party at Janelle's on Saturday," Nina asked. "I need to know what happened."

Jair was quiet for a moment. It was almost as if he were trying to think of how to answer.

"Nah, not really," he said.

"Not *really*?" Nina repeated. "What does that mean? Were you there or not?"

"Uh, it means not really," Jair said firmly. "Why?"

"No one seems to know what went on. I thought you might have been there and would know the details."

Jair had an odd look on his face. "Can't help you," he said.

Nina didn't totally believe what he was saying. "So what *did* you do Saturday night?" she asked. She tried to sound friendly, but somehow it came out like an accusation.

Jair hesitated again. "Oh, not much," he said. "Hung out, mostly."

"Hung out where?" Nina pressed.

"Here and there," Jair said vaguely.

This wasn't like Jair. Usually he liked to show how much he knew about school events. He always put himself in the middle of anything that happened.

"Whatever," she said, walking away.

She heard loud crying coming from another table. Brennay Baxter was sitting with some friends, who were trying to console her.

Nina knew Brennay and Thomas were

sometimes a couple. She turned toward that table and pulled out her notebook.

"I heard Thomas was in an accident," she said to Brennay. "What can you tell me? Were you there?"

Brennay began sobbing again. Her friends told Nina the story. Thomas and Brennay had had a fight, so she hadn't gone to the party. Now her boyfriend was under arrest, and her best friend was in the hospital. Brennay wailed that it was all her fault.

Nina wrote down the details. Knowing Brennay's reputation for jealousy, she wondered what bothered Brennay the most: her boyfriend's arrest, her best friend's injuries, or the fact that they were together.

After lunch, Nina headed for health class. When she walked in, she saw Charlie Ray and Neecy Bethune talking to Ms. Billingsley.

As soon as the bell rang, Ms. Billingsley held up her hand to get the class quiet.

"Class, I've just learned that one of you actually had an opportunity to practice what we've been learning," she said.

Nina looked around.

"Jair, can you tell us what happened Saturday night?" Ms. Billingsley continued.

Nina whirled around to look at Jair.

"It was no big deal," he said. "Some guy was choking on a piece of pizza. I did that thing we learned and it popped out."

"Sounds like a big deal to me!" Ms. Billingsley said. "Anything you want to share about how it worked? Anything that might help someone else in the future?"

"Only thing is, I wasn't sure where to squeeze him," Jair said. "Like I could do it wrong or something. But since all I wanted to do was get what was stuck to pop out, it didn't matter if it was perfect or anything."

"Great point," Ms. Billingsley said. "And how did you feel when you were done?"

"Hungry," Jair said. "My pizza was getting cold!"

The class laughed. "Well, you have reason to be very proud of yourself," Ms. Billingsley said. "And I'm proud of you too. And just for that, you don't have to do tonight's homework. You've earned yourself an A."

"For the class?" Jair said, surprised.

"No, for tonight's homework," Ms. Billingsley said, smiling. "Now, let's get to work."

Nina shook her head. She couldn't believe Jair hadn't told her about this when she spoke with him earlier. He had saved the guy's life, but he kept it to himself.

Amazing.

CHAPTER 22

JAIR

Jair felt all warm inside. He was so glad that Neecy and Charlie had seen him help the guy who was choking. He didn't have to tell anyone what he had done. Someone else told the story for him. Being humble felt good.

He felt the way he had after Janelle's party so long ago. Like everyone thought he was a good guy. He wanted to feel that way all the time. But not from stealing stuff and then turning it in. Or from setting a fire and then discovering it. It may have looked to others like he was doing something heroic, but he knew the truth. That was fake.

This felt different.

This was real.

He thought he might ask his uncle if

police officers felt this way all the time. He was intrigued by the idea of joining the police. Or maybe being in the military. Something where he felt he was helping people.

He looked over at Melinda. She looked back at him and smiled. He wondered why he hadn't thought she was pretty before. He looked around the room. Melinda was one of the prettiest girls at Cap Central.

He didn't know where things were going with Melinda. He didn't know whether the police academy was the right place for him. He didn't know if he wanted to join the military.

So many unanswered questions.

But it didn't matter.

He felt good.

Leslie McGill

CAP CENTRAL
series

FIGHTER

978-1-62250-705-4

RUNNING SCARED

978-1-62250-706-1

HACKER

978-1-62250-707-8

GEARHEAD

978-1-68021-044-6

THE GAME

978-1-68021-045-3

HERO

978-1-68021-046-0

ABOUT THE AUTHOR

Leslie McGill was raised in Pittsburgh. She attended Westminster College (Pa.) and American University in Washington, D.C. She lives in Silver Spring, Maryland, a suburb of Washington, D.C., where she works in a middle school. She lives with her husband, a newspaper editor, and has two adult children.

WANT TO READ MORE URBAN TITLES?

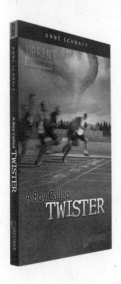

Turn the page for a sneak peek at Anne Schraff's Urban Underground title: *A Boy Called Twister*.

ISBN: 978-1-61651-002-2

CHAPTER ONE

Kevin Walker walked slowly onto the campus of Harriet Tubman Senior High School. The school was bigger than any other he'd ever attended. Right in front of the building was a large statue of a woman in a long dress with high button shoes and a cape. She had a determined look on her plain, kind face.

"That's Harriet Tubman," a girl offered. "Our school is named for her."

"Oh," Kevin said.

"She led a lot of slaves to freedom in the eighteen hundreds. They called it the 'Underground Railroad.' It wasn't a railroad, though. It was a string of safe houses where the slaves hid in the daytime. The slave catchers were after them with dogs and everything. So they traveled by night and hid during the day," the girl explained with a smile. "You're a new student, huh?"

"Yeah. I just moved here from Texas. Oh, my name is Kevin Walker," Kevin said.

"I'm Alonee Lennox," the girl introduced herself. "Welcome to Tubman High. It's a good school. We got some great teachers and some okay ones. Lot of friendly kids. That's what I love about Tubman."

Kevin nodded. The girl seemed nice enough—friendly to be sure. Kevin tended to be shy, and he smiled and thanked her and then moved on. Kevin felt uncomfortable talking to people he didn't know, or maybe to anybody. Before moving to Tubman, he and his mother had lived in a small town in Texas, Spurville. His mother was a registered nurse. There were just the two of them. Kevin had gone to Spurville High School, which was about one-fourth the size of Tubman. While Tubman had trees and a nice green lawn, Spurville High was shabby without much landscaping. Still, Kevin missed it. He missed everything about Spurville. He felt like a fish out of water, having trouble breathing.

Kevin looked at his class schedule. He had English first. In Spurville Mrs. Roberts, an elderly woman, taught English. It was Kevin's favorite class. On hot days she put out a bowl of lemonade with ice floating in it, and the students were welcome to dip in and fill their paper cups. Kevin read the name of the teacher here: Mr. Pippin. He wondered what he was like. Probably he wouldn't be as nice as Mrs. Roberts.

When Kevin walked into the classroom, he felt many eyes on him. He was arriving in the middle of the school year, which was uncommon. He wasn't dressed like the other guys in the room. Instead of the new styles, he wore old jeans and a white shirt. He didn't see anybody else wearing a white shirt. Everybody else wore T-shirts. But Kevin's grandmother insisted he wear a nicely pressed white shirt.

Kevin heard snickering when he sat down. He saw three boys staring at him and laughing. Kevin's face warmed. He wished he were back in Spurville. Twenty times a day he wished that, but he couldn't go back to Spurville until he finished high school. He wouldn't have minded being here in California for a visit, but to think

Spurville was not home anymore made him sick to the core of his being.

Kevin noticed the girl who told him about Harriet Tubman was in this class too. She smiled at him, and she seemed worried about him. Kevin knew who Harriet Tubman was even before Alonee explained her importance. Kevin had listened out of politeness. Kevin's mother taught him a lot of things, including the story of the "Black Moses," Harriet Tubman's nickname.

Mr. Pippin appeared at the front desk, sliding in like a gray ghost. Kevin liked him immediately. He was old and worn looking. His suit was shabby. Kevin thought he must have a lot of knowledge, like Mrs. Roberts did. Kevin and Mr. Pippin had something else in common too. Kevin was nervous being in this classroom, and for some reason Mr. Pippin seemed uneasy too.

"We will be discussing 'The Rocking-Horse Winner' today," Mr. Pippin announced. "A fine story by D. H. Lawrence. Does anyone wish to start?"

A boy in the back of the room rocked back and forth in his chair, making a squeaking noise.

"Marko Lane," Mr. Pippin said, "stop that."

"I was trying to get into the mood of the story, Mr. Pippin, you know, the rocking horse," Marko replied. His friends laughed.

Kevin felt sorry for the teacher, who looked stressed. Mr. Pippin looked like an outnumbered soldier on the battlefield, bravely fighting on though he knew in the end he was doomed. Kevin was shy in social situations, but he liked to participate in class discussions. He was articulate when he had something to say. By a happy coincidence, Mrs. Roberts had introduced her English class to the "Rocking-Horse Winner" a few weeks ago in Spurville. So Kevin raised his hand.

"The story has a very powerful message about how needing more and more money can destroy people," Kevin stated.

Mr. Pippin stared at the new boy.

The dead, dull look in the teacher's face flamed with a look of hope. "Yes! Give us an example of this ..."—he consulted the roster—"Kevin."

"Well," Kevin went on. "The mother. She never felt she had enough money. She was driven to search for more. And this destroyed her son."

"The mother," Alonee added, "felt the family was unlucky because they didn't have more money."

"Yes, yes," Mr. Pippin said.

"Even the walls seemed to be crying for more money," Jaris Spain, another student, offered.

"Yes, yes," Mr. Pippin encouraged. A real class discussion was going on, and Kevin had started it.

Marko Lane moved his desk with a scraping noise. Usually that kind of antic brought laughter from his friends. But now it seemed everybody wanted to talk about the story.

"The boy in the story—Paul," Mr. Pippin interjected. "How did his mother's obsession with success affect him?"

"He like caught the disease of wanting more money for his mother's sake," Kevin answered. "He rode that wooden rocking horse in his room, and he got the names of real horses, and he bet on them and won money for his mom. And eventually he died riding that horse."

When the class ended, Kevin decided he really liked Mr. Pippin. He reminded Kevin of

Mrs. Roberts. He was an interesting, intelligent man.

As Kevin walked from class, Marko Lane stuck out his foot and made Kevin stumble. Then Marko said with exaggerated concern, "Hey, I'm sorry dude. I didn't see you."

"It's okay," Kevin muttered.

"Where you from, man?" Marko asked.

"Texas," Kevin replied. He walked a little faster. He hoped to lose Marko Lane and the boys who trailed along with him.

"Texas!" Marko repeated. "I never met anybody from Texas before." He looked at his friends and asked them if they knew anybody from Texas. They shook their heads, laughing. Marko was on top of his game.

"You got a whole lot of cows down there, don't you man?" Marko asked.

"Uh, not where I lived," Kevin said.

"Then how come you smell like cow pies?" Marko asked, causing an eruption of laughter from his friends. "Not to offend you or anything dude, but I think you been spending too much time on the range."

Kevin knew they were baiting him, but he

ignored them. He saw a teacher just ahead. At least he thought she was a teacher—a smartly dressed woman carrying a briefcase. He hurried to catch up to her, "Excuse me, ma'am, where's Room 24?" he asked, "I got American history there."

The woman was beautiful. She smiled at Kevin and said, "I'm going there now. I teach the class. I'm Torie McDowell. And you are—"

"Kevin Walker," Kevin responded. He glanced back and saw Marko and his friends falling back into the shadows. For some reason they seemed afraid of this woman.

"Welcome to Tubman High, Kevin. We just go around this corner and we're there," Ms. McDowell said.

Kevin took a seat in the middle of the classroom. He was glad not to see Marko Lane and his buddies. Back in Spurville, there were boys like Marko. Kevin developed a deep hatred for them. He tried to avoid them, but sometimes things got too bad. Then Kevin had to deal with them.

Once Kevin Walker almost killed a boy. He hoped it would never get that far with Marko Lane.